I0668821

QUESTION OF TRUST

Melissa Lynn Christian

VANDO PUBLISHING
2018

Question of Trust.
© 2018 Melissa Lynn Christian. All Rights Reserved.

No part of this publication may be reproduced, stored in a retrieval system, or transmitted in any form or by any means, electronic, mechanical, recording or otherwise, without the prior written permission of the author.

ISBN: 978-0-692-12893-0
Published by Vando Publishing
Edited by V. Feisty

MelissaLynnChristian.com

The characters and events in this book are fictitious. Any similarity to real persons, living or dead, is coincidental and not intended by the author. Author is not responsible for injuries caused by readers reenacting scenes described herein.

CONTENTS

FOREWORD

IN THIS BOOK, you will see that I write about a dungeon in Chapter 17. In that chapter, you will see that I use capitalization and lowercase in a way that is not grammatically or editorially correct. I did it this way to express proper "lifestyle" respect. Whenever talking about the Dominant, in the beginning or middle of a sentence, they are to be capitalized. Accordingly, when referring to a submissive, they are always lowercase. When I refer to a group that is comprised of both Dominants and submissives, you will see the combination of upper and lowercase letters beginning the words.

In that chapter you will also take notice that Debra is referred to with upper and lowercase letters. In this case, it represents which position she is playing at the time because she is what they refer to as a switch, both Dominant and submissive.

CHAPTER 1

A S THEY DROVE through the myriad of roads to exit the airport, he kissed her hand many times. There were no other sounds in the car. Daniel was the first to break the silence.

"Would you like to tell me about your time in LA?"

Stephanie turned in her seat to face him, "It was unlike anything I could have ever imagined. I met some wonderful people. I think I can use them to further the business."

"That is a good thing, but what about your time with Zach?" Daniel questioned.

"My time with Zachary was... very interesting."

"I would have thought you were on a short name basis with him by now," he said.

"I would not consider it being casual. Yes, we did have some fun while I was there, but this is business. I can't skew the line. I need to be focused and not get caught up in feelings. We have an advertising contract with him and he may want a spokesperson deal as well."

"How did you leave things?"

She didn't have a good answer; they really did not discuss the financial side of the additional option. "We will need to negotiate with him. I don't have a solid figure right now."

"Are you going to handle that yourself?"

She thought about that for a minute, "I think I will leave that up to the accountant. That is his job."

Daniel chuckled, "Yes, yes it is, but I know how you like to be in control."

She looked at him, brow raised, "Oh, really?"

They both laughed, each knowing that she did have areas in her life where she had to be in control, but the bedroom was not one of them.

"Umm, wasn't that our exit?" Stephanie asked.

"It would be if we were going home."

"O…K… where are we going?"

"It's a surprise. I've been thinking about a few things lately and came up with a solution."

"A solution to what?"

"I can't tell you or I would ruin the surprise."

He needed to divert her attention. He lifted their hands to her face. He brushed against her cheek, stuck his pointer finger straight and ran it over the outline of her lips. He pushed his finger between her lips. She brought her other hand up to meet their entanglement and began sucking his finger as though it was his cock. Mission accomplished.

She removed the entwined hand from his, grabbing his hand with both of hers, slowly moving the finger in and out of her mouth.

Her moans began. His middle finger joined the first in her warm, wet opening. Her hips started gyrating in the seat.

He took his hand from her, dragging his fingers down her chin, then her neck. He unbuttoned the first two buttons of her shirt, slid his hand into her bra, and found her hard nipple.

"I see I haven't lost my touch," he said softly.

"No, that's not possible," she said in a very breathy voice. She was squirming and moaning. She moved in her seat in order to open her legs.

"Good girl," Daniel whispered as he slid his hand from her knee, up her thigh, to her underwear. He wedged two fingers between her skin and panties. He pushed them between her lips to find her clit awaiting his touch.

He began rubbing her sensitive spot. Her legs spread further as she turned in her seat. Her moans were audible and rising in pitch. He manipulated the flesh until she was nearly screaming.

On the verge of an orgasm, he slid his fingers into her pussy, pumping her to climax.

She was grabbing the seat and dash when the explosion of

ecstasy flooded over her body. She couldn't hold back the screams of delight that followed. He continued fucking her with his fingers until the tension released from her body.

When she relaxed, he took his fingers and placed them in his mouth. Pulling them out, he said, "I love the way you taste."

She was trying to straighten herself in the seat. "Thank you, baby."

She had not noticed that they had gotten off the main highway and were now on a rural road heading into the mountains. She took his hand in hers and looked out the window at the breathtaking scenery laid out in front of them.

"I don't think I'm familiar with this area," she said, breaking the silence.

"It's a gorgeous area. Very secluded. The only people traveling here—live here."

"This could be trouble," she giggled as she said the words.

"I hope it is."

They drove quietly for a few minutes before Daniel turned down a long driveway. The lane meandered through the trees and underbrush. They came to an opening where an A-frame style home had been built.

Daniel placed the car in park and turned it off. "What do you think?"

"It's adorable. Is it yours?

"This is *our* escape."

She cocked her head, not knowing how to take this. Was this his way of committing to her? Did he just purchase this for the two of them to be together? So many questions ran through her head, but they would have to wait. Daniel had already gotten out of the car and came over to open her door.

He took her by the hand, not letting go as they walked up the three stairs and across the wooden deck to the door. With his other hand, he took the key out of his pocket and placed it in the lock. He pushed the door open, "After you."

She walked through the door and into the cabin. Looking around, she saw the kitchen off in the distance. The fireplace in the middle of the main room was adorned with candles on the mantel and a white fluffy rug surrounded by an L-shaped, deep seated, leather sofa. It was exactly what a getaway in the woods should be.

He closed the door, took her hand, flipped it palm up, and placed the key in it. "This one is yours."

She looked at him inquisitively. He ignored her and leaned in to kiss her. What began as small pecks soon grew into a deep, passionate display of affection. His arms wrapped around her, hers around his neck. Both of their breathing, now deep and slow.

He pulled back from her. She looked like a sad puppy. "Don't worry, sexy, I just want to show you around. Well," he chuckled, "there really isn't much more to see than you can from here. There are two bedrooms and a bath upstairs. Our bedroom and bath are in the back corner."

Our bedroom, she liked the sound of that. Maybe things were stepping up a notch. Could this be a glimpse of things to come? Maybe a full-blown commitment? That would be wonderful, but for now she was going to enjoy this moment.

"Before I show you our room, how about a bite to eat, maybe a glass of wine? We can talk about your trip."

She put her thoughts away, "Sure, I am a little hungry. A glass of wine would be great. I just hope it doesn't make me fall asleep."

They both began to laugh. Sleep was not in the plan, at least not right away. Daniel went into the kitchen, Stephanie following, her head twisting and turning, taking everything in.

"This place is adorable. How long have you had it?"

"There were a bunch of guys and I who have had it for many years. It was our place to go to get away from our wives."

"It's decorated well for a bunch of guys."

"Oh, believe me, when the guys and I had it, it looked nothing like this. I bought them out after my divorce and remodeled it the way I wanted. The guys would not even recognize it today."

"They don't still have keys, right?"

He put her glass of wine in front of her, "No, gorgeous, they don't have keys. No one will walk in on us."

She put the key on the counter and picked up her wine glass. He grabbed the plate of cheese he was cutting and walked into the living room. There was an ottoman by the sofa where Daniel put the plate. They sat on the sofa facing each other and began to talk.

"I have to say, this was the strangest trip I could have ever imagined. Sometimes I swear life is stranger than fiction."

They both laughed. "Well, you do seem to have the most interesting things happen to you. My life seems very mundane compared to yours."

She cocked her head and gave him the look. "Seriously? Might I remind you who it was that started this crazy train?"

"Crazy? I thought you liked it?" he said as he raised the glass to his lips.

"I will admit it is very interesting, but I'm not sure how this is helping me."

"It's not hurting you financially."

"That's true. I hope this trip adds to the financial part."

"Yes, now tell me about the sex part of the trip."

"I don't recall saying there was sex."

"You did, in a round-about way." She looked at him, puzzled. "You said—fun, dungeon, party, interesting. I know those are code words for sex."

"Okay, yes there was a bit of that."

"Tell me."

"Where do I begin? Well, in the dungeon he tied me to a cross and used some of his toys."

"Which toys did he use and how?"

"He began with a large, veined dildo. He used that while I was lying on the table, before the cross."

Daniel adjusted his cock. He was becoming aroused.

"You know how I have that favorite vibrator that has the clit stimulation?"

"Yes, I know it well."

"He followed the dildo with that one. He held it in place until I couldn't take it any longer, I had to pull away."

"How did that go over?"

"Not well. He took out his cock and shoved it down my throat."

"Down your throat, so he must be large."

"He is well endowed."

"Is his dick better than mine?"

"Of course not, there is no cock better than yours. Yours is the only one that satisfies me." She leaned toward him and kissed him on the lips.

"Go on." Daniel opened his pants and took his manhood out, stroking it as she spoke.

"It was after that when I was placed on the cross. He used a vibrating butt plug in my ass then put the vibrator back in my cunt. I couldn't get away. He cranked them up and I nearly lost my mind. I have never been so close to passing out. The only thing that saved me was the batteries dying down."

"Did you squirt for him?"

"Yes, many times. I felt like a fountain. After he removed the vibrator from my pussy, he then used his fingers and pounded me until I squirted again. I was completely drained. He released me from the cross, put me back on the table, and fucked me hard until he came."

"I do enjoy hearing your stories." Daniel commented as he continued to play with his rod. "I can't decide if I want to hear more, or make my own."

Stephanie placed her glass on the floor. She knelt on the sofa and took his cock in her hand. She placed her tongue as low as she could on the shaft and licked to the tip. Daniel reclined and gave her complete access. She licked it a few more times before taking just the head into her mouth.

She sucked it gently, rolled her tongue over it as she did. She popped the head in and out from between her lips mocking the way he would tease her pussy. He began to moan softly. She continued her pattern a few moments before unexpectedly driving her lips to meet his pants.

"Ahhhh, fuck… that is amazing!"

She kept in place, turning her head, twisting on his manhood. She pulled back, never allowing his dick to leave her mouth, and began forcefully moving it in and out. He allowed her a few minutes before he grabbed her hair and pulled her from his cock.

"Let's take this in the bedroom."

She waited next to the couch as he stood and buttoned his pants. He took her hand and walked her through the short hallway and into their bedroom. There was a tall poster bed against the far wall.

As they walked in the room, he began removing her clothes with an unusual swiftness. He quickly unbuttoned the remaining buttons before throwing her blouse on a chair, her skirt was just hurriedly pushed to the floor, her bra found the nightstand. The only thing left was her panties.

He faced her toward the bed, then pushed her head into the mattress. He opened his pants and let them drop. Pushing his boxer briefs to his knees, he grabbed her hips, slid her panties to the slide, and lined up his dick to her cunt.

"Are you ready to be fucked properly?"

"Yes."

"Yes, what?"

"Yes, Master."

She spread her legs further as his head explored her hole. He pulled on her hips and thrust his groin toward her, driving his shaft deep inside.

Her scream was a combination surprise and pain. It was unusual for him to drive so far, so fast. He wasted no time pounding her pussy.

"Is my cock better than his?"

"Of course it is."

He continued to ride her, moving from her hips to using her tits as his anchor, grabbing her nipples and pinching them. He pulled his cock from her, tore her from the bed, and dropped her to her knees.

As she turned toward him, she saw him stroking his cock. "Open your mouth."

She opened her mouth and waited for his warm cum to project from his tip.

"Catch as much as you can and show it to me."

She shook her head in acknowledgement. A few strokes later, the white cream was spewing from his dick. She felt it on her eyelid, some dropped on her breast. He got closer and finished draining his jizz into her mouth.

She kept her mouth open, her tongue white with protein. "Good girl, you can swallow."

He pulled up his trousers and went into the bathroom, coming back with a warm wash cloth. She took it from him, then wiped her face and chest.

She was confused by his actions. He had never reacted in this way before. Did she do something wrong? Their relationship was open, and he typically encouraged her to be with other men. The stories always excited him, but this time was different. She felt the anger within the entanglement. Where was this going?

Daniel reached out his hand and helped her from the floor.

"I think we should go finish our drinks."

He helped gather her clothes. She dressed as he quickly threw on his pants and left to go back into the living room.

CHAPTER 2

A S SHE DRESSED, her mind went over their encounter. It was so out of the ordinary. Yes, their sex had always been rough and tumble, but this, this was different. This time it was fueled by anger and possibly a little punishment.

She checked her hair and make-up in the mirror. Could she have done something wrong? Could he possibly want to close this relationship? Could her commitment be around the corner? She could only hope.

She turned from the mirror and walked out into the great room. Daniel was in the kitchen refilling their glasses and getting a bit more food.

She gingerly lowered herself onto the sofa, glad she was not wearing pants. Her pussy was tender.

Daniel walked over to her, bringing a tray this time. He placed it on the ottoman before sitting on the edge of the sofa. He grabbed both glasses and pushed himself back, handing her a glass.

He looked into her eyes as he clinked his glass to hers, "Here is to a new chapter in both of our lives."

She smiled before taking a sip of her wine. This was a step toward them becoming the couple she patiently longed for. Her eyes began to glaze over. The look of love was written all over her face.

"You have a wonderful afterglow," he said with a smile. "What are your plans for the week?"

"I will be working. I need to meet with Maggie tomorrow and go over the details. She has been working on a campaign for a few signings in the area. I need to spend some time with my daughter. That's about everything."

"No men in your plans?"

"None other than you; if you have the time."

"That is actually what I was getting around to. I thought maybe we could come here this weekend. We could get here Saturday, late morning, and head home Sunday, late afternoon."

A stunned look came over her face, so he added, "I know it's not much, but it's a start."

Tears began to well up in her eyes. "That is the best idea you have ever had."

She leaned in and gave him a hug and kiss. This would be the first time they spent an extended amount of time together. She had never pushed, she always understood that their time together was limited, but she had wanted this for months.

As she pulled back, a tear rolled down her cheek.

Wiping the tear, he said, "Baby, I didn't mean to upset you."

"It's not a bad thing. I'm very happy we will be doing this. Dare I ask what to bring?"

"I'm guessing you mean clothes? When we are here, you won't need much. We might go out for dinner Saturday evening, so a nice little something would be good. I don't know of any nudist colonies around here that have fine dining."

They chuckled. Stephanie said, "I see… so you *do* know of nudist colonies, just not ones with fine dining."

"You know me, never tell my secrets."

"You are Fort Knox. Maybe one day you will let me in." She knew there was a lot more to this man than what she had been told. Maybe one day see would earn his trust and he would allow her past those gates.

"A gentleman never kisses and tells."

"It's not the kissing I care about."

They laughed again. Their relationship was very light hearted. When they were together, they were very much at ease.

They sat on the sofa talking, nibbling, and sipping until their glasses were empty.

"I would get us another, but I think you should get home to your daughter."

They stood and he took the tray to the kitchen.

"Yes, she should be home by now. I can't wait to hear what I missed."

Ah, the triumphs and tribulations of the teen years. She was so glad to be hearing about them instead of living them out. Things had certainly changed in the years since she was in school, but the basis dynamic was still the same. This one said something about that one. This one stole that one's boyfriend. Yada, yada, yada.

Daniel washed the few dishes as Stephanie dried. She hung the towel back on the rack and began walking out of the kitchen.

Daniel picked her key off the counter and asked, "Did you forget something?"

She gasped, "Yes, I did. I guess I will get used to having this soon. I will guard it with my life."

"Honey, it's not that important."

Maybe to him it was just a key, but to her it was the precipice of her most sacred wish. He was everything she wanted in a partner. Handsome, funny, great in bed, and he was the one that could keep her safe.

They walked to the porch. Stephanie quickly turned back to catch another glimpse of the cabin before Daniel shut the door. The few short steps to the car felt like they were walked on air.

Daniel opened her door, and she slid in. While he walked around the car, Stephanie took out her phone and added the location into her maps.

As he closed his car door, Daniel saw her putting down the phone. "Ahh, I knew it was too good to be true. You were without that phone for quite some time, anything good?"

"Oh, I didn't even check messages. I was mapping the location for future reference."

"Now honey, you don't have to worry about that. I will be with you every time you are here. We have seen the occasional bear, and I would not want you to get hurt."

It was very sweet of him to be concerned for her wellbeing. Just like she knew, he would keep her safe.

She settled into the seat and peered out the window, once again taking in the scenery.

♦

"Honey, you are home."

She felt a gentle touch on her arm as she came out of her little nap. She had once again fallen fast asleep. This was unlike her. Zachary had certainly done a number. Or maybe this was what she had needed for so long. No matter the cause, she knew tonight would be an early evening.

Daniel took her things out of the trunk as she got out of the car. "Do you mind if I walk you in?"

"Why would I ever mind?"

"You had said that your daughter would be home. I'm sure she will be excited to see you, me, not so much."

They chuckled. "I'm sure she is in her room and will not take notice that I am home until I go up and get her. Or send her a text."

"I guess you are right. Things are so different now."

"No need to tell me, it's my life."

Stephanie opened the front door and they both went inside, Daniel closing the door behind them. He placed her things by the staircase and took her into his arms.

"I missed you very much. I'm glad you are back in my arms. Saturday can't get here soon enough."

"I know. Thank you."

He gave her a long kiss, ran his hands through her hair, kissed her on the forehead, and walked to the door.

Turning the knob, he looked back at her and said, "I will pick you up at 10 Saturday morning. Don't bring much."

She smiled and said, "Don't worry I won't. I'll see you then."

"Yes you will. Good bye, gorgeous."

"Good bye, handsome."

He closed the door. She turned toward the stairs, looked at her bags, and sighed. There was no time like the present to lug them up the stairs and then see her daughter.

She grabbed the two bags and began the climb. The stairs seemed longer than before. She was drained, emotionally and physically. She walked into her room and placed the bags next to her dresser. She walked across the hall to her daughter's closed door.

A quick knock before turning the knob; she walked in to find her daughter on the bed, earbuds in, listening to a podcast while doodling. She took a few steps into the room before her daughter nearly leapt off the bed with a scream.

"Why did you do that?"

"I didn't do anything."

"Yes you did. You came in here without knocking and scared me half to death. You could have at least sent me a text that you were back, but no why would you do something like that?"

"You're right, I should have told you I was back, but I did tell you I would be home today. And I did knock."

"Well you should have known that I would be wearing earbuds when you didn't hear any noise."

"Yes, I am the worst mother in the world. I abandon my daughter for days. Don't leave any food in the house. She has no vehicle to get anywhere. I should be tarred and feathered." Stephanie always tried to calm the situation with sarcasm.

"Haha, well at least you are back in time to go to the parent meeting tonight."

"Ugh, I completely forgot. When do we have to be there?"

"We need to leave in an hour, unless we want to grab something to eat, then we need to leave now."

Stephanie thought about that for a second before saying, "Okay, let's go get something to eat. How about the little diner on the way to school? They are usually fast, and I like the salad bar."

"That's fine. Just give me a minute."

Stephanie went out of the room and back downstairs. She quickly glanced at her phone to check messages. There were three. She decided to answer one of them.

Zachary:

Hope all went well with your ride home. I am sure your daughter missed you greatly, I know I will. The remainder of my trip was uneventful. I'm on the ranch. I hope you enjoy your time at home.

Stephanie messaged back:

I just returned home, and I'm not sure if my daughter missed me. It sounded as though you were in for a very enjoyable week. Make the best of your time with your friends. I wish you a safe flight home.

Stephanie had heard her daughter hurrying down the bare wooden stairs. As she looked up from her phone she saw her daughter standing in front of her, waiting to leave.

"Okay, I'm ready to go," Stephanie said to Brianna as she grabbed her purse and keys. They walked into the garage, pressing the opener as they passed by.

In the car Stephanie began the conversation. "So, why don't you tell me what I missed?'

"You didn't miss much. Everyone was quiet the past couple of days. A few of my friends are beginning to pick colleges to tour."

"Ugh, I don't know if I am ready for that. Do you have any that you want to see?"

"Not really. I'm waiting to hear from my friends about their visits before I decide. There is plenty of time."

"It will be here before you know it. My head is still spinning that we are even at this point in your life."

"Don't even go getting all mushy about this. You've known it was coming. This should not be a surprise. I can't wait!"

Stephanie smiled. "You have no idea what you are in for. Classes are harder, we know how you love your AP classes now. You will be sharing a bedroom, smaller than yours, with someone else. You will share the showers with who knows how many others. It's not going to be easy balancing your new friends and your school work. You need to remember why you are there."

"God, I should have just let you cry. It would have saved me a lecture."

"It's not a lecture; it's… a dose of reality. Certain things look much better from the outside."

"Really, mother. Like there has never been anything in my life that has turned out to be worse than it looked."

Stephanie paused, thinking about the past few years. It had not been easy and Brianna had been such a trouper. She had a couple breakdowns, but nothing she didn't recover from quickly. Stephanie hated to admit it, but Brianna was so much more advanced than Stephanie had been at her age. She knew college would be a slight challenge, but Brianna would take it in stride.

They pulled into the parking lot of the diner. Stephanie took the closest spot to park the car. They grabbed their purses and headed inside.

There was a lovely young lady as hostess this evening. She was smiling as they walked in. She asked if it would be two for dinner. They both shook their heads and said, "Yes." They followed her to a booth in the middle of the outside wall. After the menus were placed on the table, Stephanie and Brianna slid into the benches.

They each picked up their menu and began perusing the pages. So many options.

Stephanie was not sure what she was hungry for, "What do you think you are going to have?"

Brianna was flipping between two pages. "I'm not sure if I want a burger or some pasta."

Neither of those things sounded like the option for Stephanie. She kept flipping.

A waitress walked to their table. "What can I get you ladies to drink?"

Stephanie wanted a Coke, and Brianna decided to have a Dr. Pepper.

"Any appetizers?"

"Mozzarella sticks, please," Brianna answered.

"Okay, an appetizer for you ma'am?"

Stephanie shook her head no.

"Let me put the order in and I will be right back with your drinks."

They all smiled. They went back to looking at the menus without another word. Flipping through the pages, Stephanie finally set it down and sat back with a sigh. Across from her was a young lady ready to face the next chapter in her life. The two of them were very similar, just decades apart.

Brianna looked up from her menu to see her mother staring at her. "What is wrong now?"

"Nothing. Can't a mother look at her daughter?"

"That depends who the mother is. You think crazy thoughts."

Stephanie laughed, "I think crazy thoughts? You are being a bit dramatic, don't you think?"

"No."

"I was just thinking about all the changes that are about to happen for you. Leaving high school, leaving home, experiencing the real world. It's a pretty big deal."

"It's not that big a deal. Everybody is using these college tours as extra days off from school. I don't know how serious they really take them. Did I tell you Amanda scheduled to see nine colleges?"

"Nine? Have her parents lost their minds? That's just crazy. I can't see needing to visit more than three."

"Her parents have nothing better to do with their money."

"Must be nice."

At that moment, their waitress returned to the table with their drinks. "Have you ladies decided?"

They shook their heads. Stephanie ordered the soup and salad bar, while Brianna ordered a chicken Caesar wrap. The waitress told Stephanie to feel free to get her salad, then left for the kitchen.

"I'll be right back," Stephanie said as she scooted out of the booth and over to the salad bar. She filled the plate with her normal array of vegetables, cheese, salads, and dressing. When she returned to the table, Brianna was deep into her phone, answering texts and searching social media. This was going to be a quiet dinner.

They made quick work of their meals. Being limited to a specific arrival time, they had no time for lingering. They got the check, paid the bill, and hurried to the car.

It took ten minutes to get to the school, giving them five minutes before they would be late. Stephanie was not worried. This teacher never started any meeting on time. They walked into the auditorium and sat in seats near the back.

A couple minutes later, Brianna's friend Josie and her father came over. Josie sat with Brianna, her father was left asking Stephanie if she minded him sitting next to her. He was an attractive man, who would possibly mind?

Stephanie and Josie's dad exchanged niceties before waiting quietly for the meeting to begin. The girls, they were not so quiet, chatting up a storm before the meeting and whispering occasionally during it.

Both parents sent daggers to them with their eyes during the meeting as they felt the girls were getting too loud. When the meeting ended, everyone said their good-byes and headed to their cars.

As chatty as Brianna had been with Josie, she was just as quiet on the drive home.

CHAPTER 3

I T HAD BEEN A LONG DAY. Brianna went to her room upon arriving home. The house was quiet. Stephanie poured herself a glass of wine and took her phone from her purse before going into the living room.

She sat in the chair, placing her glass on the end table and turning on the lamp. She checked her phone for messages. There was one from Maggie, her PR advisor, reminding her of their 9 am meeting. A couple of girlfriends had messaged to see how the trip went and Zachary had responded to her last text.

How odd that Daniel was quiet. He must have had some important meeting. Maybe he thought she had been relaxing, since she had not messaged him all night. No worries, all was wonderful between them.

She sat in the chair thinking about the big step they had taken this afternoon with her introduction to the cabin. Maybe he had realized how much he cared for her while she was gone. Could there possibly be a little jealousy? He had always said he was not a jealous man, but was that true? These actions seemed to suggest otherwise.

The thoughts of their relationship warmed her. Yes, she played along with his "open relationship" game, but inside she wanted a commitment. She wanted them to be the alpha couple others looked up to. Together they could be very powerful. He fueled her, and she hoped she fueled him. Imagine the heights they could climb together as a couple. In her mind, there was no stopping them.

A few more sips of wine added to the warmth, especially between her legs. She began to fidget in her seat. The nerves in her clit were heightened by the alcohol. Her movements made her thong rub between her lips. The sensation was maddening.

She continued grinding her seat. She placed a finger over her panties and added stimulation. She continued stirring her clit even more swiftly until at last, her orgasm climaxed and she was once again able to relax.

She picked up her phone and looked at Zachary's message:

LOL! Looks like you didn't enjoy our time together considering how quickly you are dropping me.

Stephanie:

I'm sorry. I didn't mean to be short with you. I just thought you would be too busy with the boys to want to have an ongoing conversation with me. BTW, I did enjoy our time together.

Stephanie placed her phone back on the table and grabbed the wine glass. Before it reached her lips, there was a message back from Zachary.

I will always make time for you. These guys swear every year that they aren't going to message their wives while they are here, but they all do. We don't drink that much that they need to be in the bathroom every 15 minutes. Lol

Stephanie:

I guess they like to talk a good game, most men do...

Zachary:

Darling, you certainly cannot be referring to me. That must be your other man.

Stephanie:

Haha Such a silly boy.

Zachary:

Boy? I doubt a boy could have done to you what I did. And no boy will take care of you like I can.

Take care of her? She wasn't looking for someone to take care of her. How condescending.

I am sure you take care of your women very well. I'm exhausted, I need to head to bed. Good night.

Zachary:

Good night my sweet princess. Sleep well.

His sweet princess? WTF? She needed to make sure that he

did not get carried away with his thoughts. She was not his anything. Well, okay, she was going to be his spokesperson, but that was as far as it was going. She would have to be very careful to stand her ground and not let him get carried away in his thoughts.

She let the messages for her friends go until tomorrow. She really was tired and knew if she responded to those, she would be up all night.

She finished her glass of wine, placed it in the sink and headed to bed. As she was washing her face, she began thinking about Daniel not messaging her. What could he possibly be doing all evening? He could have at least sent a little "hello."

She plugged her phone into the charger on her nightstand. After she set her alarm, she sent a text to Daniel:

Good night, handsome.

She placed the phone on the nightstand and fell asleep as soon as her head hit the pillow.

CHAPTER 4

THE SOUND OF THE ALARM woke Stephanie from a very deep sleep. She shut it off and pulled the covers closer to her chin. She really was not ready for the day. It felt so good to once again be in her own bed, she really didn't want to leave it.

Her eyes were heavy when the familiar ding of a text message from Daniel startled her. She took the phone from the nightstand and read the message:

Good morning gorgeous. I was out late last night playing cards with the guys. Didn't mean to ignore your message. How are your lips this morning?

Stephanie:

Good morning handsome. I turned in early. It was wonderful to sleep in my own bed. My lips are feeling lonely.

Daniel:

Bring them to mine and let me kiss them gently.

Stephanie:

Yes, Sir. Your lips on mine are such a delight. Let me run my hands through your hair.

Daniel:

Mine are intertwined in yours, pulling gently.

Stephanie:

I am so wet. Touch me more.

Daniel:

What would you like me to touch? Tell me how much you want it.

Stephanie:

I want you to touch my tits, pinch my nipples. I long for you. My body needs you. I want to cum. Please make me cum.

Daniel:

Such a naughty little girl. I will pinch your nipples before I push you to your knees. Do you feel my hardness?

Stephanie:

I do. I feel him pressing against my abdomen. He wants to be inside me. Let him loose. Let me pleasure him.

Daniel:

What do you want to do to him?

Stephanie:

I want to take him between my lips. I want to make love to him with my mouth. I want to take him deep in my throat.

Daniel:

Nice. While he is in your mouth, I will continue pinching your nipples. Don't linger too long, baby. I want your pussy riding my cock.

Stephanie:

I'll straddle your manhood and slide him deep into my wet hole. Forward or backward?

Daniel:

Backward, I want to finger your asshole.

Stephanie:

As you wish. Sliding him in. Oh, he feels so good. A perfect fit. Let me take it slow at first. I want to feel every vein on those amazing inches. The thickness fills me, stretching just a bit.

As she hit send she glanced at the time. Shit! Now she had to hurry to get ready and be at her meeting on time. She should know better by now, there is no such thing as a quickie sexting.

She threw off her pajamas and brushed her teeth, as the water warmed in the shower. This was going to have to be quick. She knew he would not need another text for a few minutes while he stroked himself to pre cum. As she rinsed the shampoo from her hair, the ding sounded again. She would get to him as soon as she was finished.

It took a couple of minutes to condition her hair and towel off. Time to check the message.

Mmmm, enjoying every stroke. You can ride him all morning.

All morning? Not today. She had to throw on some clothes and makeup. There were ten minutes standing between her being on time and being late. She grabbed clothes out of the closet and threw them on while trying to send another message.

Beginning to ride faster. On the edge of a cum. A few strokes and I will be over.

She placed moisturizer, base and powder on her face. Two minutes left. She quickly shadowed her eyes and lined them. She grabbed the mascara and lip gloss to go, easy enough for the car.

She ran down the stairs, shoes in her hand. Brianna was in the kitchen grabbing a bagel before heading to school.

"Have a great day. Do we have anything going on this evening?" Stephanie questioned.

"I might stop at Josie's after school, but nothing else."

"Okay, do I have to make dinner?"

"I don't know. Maybe we can just get pizza."

"Okay, let me know," Stephanie yelled as she hurried through the garage door and into the car.

And… the ding.

Keep going baby. Love your tits bouncing.

Fuck! She really did not have time for this right now. She pulled the car out of the garage and when she was on the road, she told her phone to text:

Going… over… the… top…drenching your balls.

A few minutes into the drive, and she began to calm down. The short interaction with Brianna had put a couple of minutes behind, but she could make it up. Ding. If only that would stop.

Love to have your juices dripping from my balls. Where do you want my cum today?

Praise be, she would finally be able to concentrate on the tasks at hand.

Cum inside my pussy.

It really was amazing how when manually putting words like—fuck, pussy, tits, cock – the phone would auto correct at times, but when using voice to text, every word was spelled perfectly. Somehow, in her mind that just did not make sense.

She was nearly at her meeting, when… ding.

Yes, baby. Hands on your hips, driving him hard into your soaked cunt. Ahhhhh, adding my juices to yours. Felt so wonderful. Have a great day.

Seriously? Have a great day? She knew he would, hers was yet to be determined.

She pulled into the parking lot, found a great space, and parked the car. She placed her phone on vibrate before exiting the car. She walked across the parking lot and into the coffee shop.

As she walked in, Maggie waived to her. She had already found them a quiet table in the corner, away from other customers, knowing she would be getting juicy tails prior to the discussion she needed to have with Stephanie.

Maggie was not just Stephanie's promoter, they were friends. They had met years ago, while they were still married. They had been there through the trials and tribulations of life, aided with either wine or coffee.

Stephanie stepped up to the counter and ordered a cup of coffee and an orange scone. She filled the cup with hazelnut flavored coffee and headed toward Maggie. She placed her tray on the table and gave Maggie a big hug before sliding into the booth.

"So tell me everything. I know you got the deal, but you did spend extra time there. What happened?" Maggie eagerly asked.

"Honestly, I could not have written what happened there." They both giggled. "You know how they say that life is stranger than fiction?"

"I know all too well."

"This would be one of those times. I am beginning to believe that all powerful men are just freaks of nature. I have never experienced anything like this with regular guys."

She shook her head and began picking at her scone before continuing. "He purposely flew to Seattle to talk to me prior to getting on the plane. He wanted to make sure that I was for real. The Mark that I was supposed to meet..."

Maggie shook her head, acknowledging she knew who Stephanie meant.

"That was actually his son and not the person I was

scheduled to meet."

"What?!?"

"Yeah, and by the way, Zachary, the one who is the actual boss, he went to college with Daniel."

"What the fuck?!? How is that possible? You're right, you could not have thought this up." Maggie was laughing, nearly choking on her coffee.

"I know, right." Stephanie chuckled. "Imagine my surprise when I met him as Debra after having him talk to me before we got on the plane… and then his limo drove me to the hotel."

"His limo picked you up at the airport? I don't remember that being on the itinerary."

"It wasn't. I was hailing a cab and this limo rolls up. I backed away from the curb, knowing it wasn't for me, he rolled down the window and asked me if I needed a ride. We had a nice conversation on the way to the hotel.

At the meeting, I stayed cool. You know there is a drastic difference between the two, so I just pretended not to know him. The conversation went well, it wasn't until after he made the commitment for advertising that he took my hand, kissed it and whispered my name in my ear."

"Well, you certainly could not have been surprised. It seems like this guy did his due diligence. Maybe he should be a PI."

They both cracked up over that comment.

"Maybe he should. He decided to then turn the meeting into a personal event. Let's just say I am much more acquainted with his products now than I was prior to the trip."

At this point, the two of them were laughing hysterically over the conversation. Maggie knew that Stephanie's life never went as planned, but this one took the cake… to date.

"So is he hung?"

"A lady never kisses and tells."

"You are no lady, and you did more than kiss it."

Over her laughter, Stephanie was able to say, "You're right, I did. He is more than amply endowed. I am very surprised the man is single. He is very attractive, very successful, and a wonderful lover."

"Sounds like you might have interest in him."

"No, that will never happen. We have a business relationship; that is all."

Maggie had seen a little sparkle in Stephanie's eye as she talked about her time with Zachary. She felt there could be a little more to him, if Stephanie only allowed it.

"Okay, I'll get the details over a bottle of wine one night. For now, I have a few things I need to discuss. I have some ideas, but they are going to take you away from your daughter and business. You need to put plans in place before I finalize things."

"Okay, if I need to hire someone in the business, I will. Brianna will understand as long as she sees me making money."

"Typical kid. Here is what I am thinking," she took a piece of paper out of a folder. "I have spoken with a few small bookstores and tentatively set up dates for you to travel and do book signings."

"Will you accompany me?"

"Some of them I will. I have a couple of conflicting dates, but not until later in the tour. By that time, you should be fine. If you need someone to go with you, we can look for a person at that time."

"That sounds perfect. I am very excited to get things underway. We were just talking about college last night. There is no way that the accounting business will be able to cover that as well. I need to have other avenues."

"This will do it. They need to see your face. You need to talk to the people, make the connection I know you can make. Once they know you, they will follow you anywhere and buy anything you write. We need the fan base."

"I know. The next year will be busy, but I have to do it. You know… there is no other option."

"Have you heard from your ex recently?"

"No, and I don't need to hear from him ever again. He has shown his true colors. Brianna knows he is a piece of shit. She doesn't want anything to do with him. Yes, her life has changed, but now I need to change it back."

"Just what I need to hear. You know I am going to push very hard. Are you ready?"

"Yes, yes I am. I have no other choice. I'm in the corner and I'm ready to come out swinging."

"Then let's do it."

They discussed the idea of how Maggie thought things should be planned. There was a bit of back and forth on dates and timeframes. Each lady voiced her expectations. They agreed to get back together in a week, by then Maggie would solidify the tour and Stephanie would double check with Brianna to be sure the dates did not interfere with anything important.

When the consultation was over, the women hugged, grabbed their trash to place in the receptacle, walked into the parking lot, and hugged again before getting into their cars.

Stephanie had a twenty-minute drive to her accounting office. Her mind raced with excitement over the upcoming tour. She had learned months ago to let Maggie do what she does and just follow. Maggie had not steered her wrong and Stephanie certainly did not have time to put these things together on her own. She knew enough to know what she didn't know. She had her forte and others had theirs, she was not about to reinvent the wheel.

As she pulled up to her office, she began changing her mindset toward her clients. She would need to place Debra back in the closet and focus on the business at hand. The office was quiet. Her part time assistant would not be in for another half an hour. Just enough time to catch up on emails.

CHAPTER 5

THE CLOCK READ 4:55 PM, as she began cleaning up her desk. It had been a typical day. Answering emails, analyzing budgets, and phone calls from anxious clients looking to expand, but unsure the time was right. Tonight she was getting out on time. She needed to go home and discuss this morning's meeting with Brianna. She had to be certain that her daughter was ready for this next step.

Her assistant walked over to the desk, "I finished the reports you needed. They are in the respective client files. Will you need me tomorrow?"

"I think I will be okay tomorrow," now would be the time to ask if Pam could be the answer to her being out of town. "I do have a question for you, would you be able to work more hours? I am going to need to be taking some time off here and there in the upcoming months, I would prefer to have you here more—rather than hiring someone else."

"That should not be an issue, but will I be able to get in touch with you if there is something that will not wait until you return?"

"Of course, you will be able to contact me any time. It looks like it might just be some long weekends. I will prepare a letter to go out to the clients giving them a heads up on the plan so we don't have anyone getting upset."

"That's a great idea. I know how some of them are if you are on the other line when they call. I can't imagine how they would react knowing you were out of town. They might have a coronary."

Stephanie shook her head, "Yes, there are those few who are very fearful. Don't worry, I will pay special attention to them and insure that they understand there is nothing we do that is such an emergency that it can't wait a couple of hours for an answer. It's nice to be needed, but sometimes…"

"Yes, I know. Well, I am going to head out. If you could give me a schedule of when you will need me, I will make sure to plan for it. Have a great weekend."

"Thank you, I have the feeling my weekend will be unforgettable."

"Hmmm, sounds like you have something planned. I hope it involves a man, you deserve a good one."

"It might…"

They laughed as Pam left the building. Stephanie finished organizing her desk before turning out the lights and heading to her car.

She pulled out her phone and sent Brianna a message that she was on her way.

As she drove home, she heard her phone ding numerous times. She pulled her car into the garage and quickly checked messages. She expected them to be from Brianna, but they weren't. Brianna had acknowledged her text about coming home, but Zachary had also sent a couple of messages. Two of them were pictures of him on a horse and then a message asking her how her day had gone.

Before she went in the house she messaged him back:

The meeting this morning went well. Maggie is organizing a book tour over the next couple of months. I am going to talk to my daughter this evening to make sure she will be okay with me being gone. I have already checked with my assistant and she is willing to take over while I am gone, so all is well and it was a very productive day.

She got out of the car, gathered her things, and walked into the house. She placed everything on the counter as she received a message.

That sounds wonderful! You will have to let me know when and where you will be, I will try to see if we can partner with some advertising. I will talk to Maggie tomorrow about that idea. Have a wonderful evening with your daughter.

Stephanie:
Thank you! Have fun with the boys.
Zachary:
Thank you! I will. It might include some libations.
Stephanie:
Might?
Zachary:
Lol

Stephanie put her phone down and began looking through the fridge for dinner options. Once again, her phone made the familiar sound. She picked up the phone expecting that Zachary had decided to continue the conversation. She was wrong, it was Daniel.

Good evening gorgeous! I hope everything went well in your meeting. I felt your lips on my cock this afternoon, such a naughty girl.
Stephanie:
Good evening handsome, how could I resist that amazing manhood? I love crawling under your desk and enjoying him. I hope I didn't interrupt the conversation you were having with your office manager.
Daniel:
I think she might have been wondering why I was so relaxed. She was taken aback when I gasped as my head hit the back of your throat.
Stephanie:
That's why I did it. She has no idea what she is missing. Imaging if she knew how many times we had sex on that desk… and the break room sofa.
Daniel:
Lol, I don't think she would ever return to work. Heading out to play a little tennis with the boys. Wish me luck.
Stephanie:
You don't need luck, you will kick their asses.
Daniel:
Thank you, babe. Have a great night!
Stephanie:
You're welcome. Enjoy!

She walked into her office and put her phone on the charger. She had spoken to both men that mattered in her life and she did not need any interruptions during dinner.

She went back to the kitchen and grabbed a few leftovers out of the fridge and began throwing dinner together. When she was nearly finished, Brianna walked into the kitchen.

"How were things at school today? Would you set the table?"

Brianna went to the cabinet and pulled out two plates. "Just a typical day. I have a lot of homework tonight. I need you to take a look at a story I am writing."

"The apple really didn't fall too far from the tree," Stephanie giggled.

Brianna stopped in her tracks, cocked her head, "Haha, I write mystery, not sex."

"Well, I guess that's a good thing. I can't imagine your teacher being happy about that," she paused. "Although, he is very attractive. When is parent night? I might need to visit him and leave a book behind."

"Don't you dare! I'm not going to tell you now."

"You know they send me emails, right."

"Yes, and I know how good you are about reading emails."

"Touché, that is something I need to work on."

Stephanie brought the food to the table and filled their plates. After she put the pots in the sink, she joined Brianna at the table.

"So I had a meeting with Maggie today. She has an idea that I need to run past you. She wants me to do a couple of book signings. I may need to go out of town for a couple of long weekends. Will you be okay with that?"

"As long as it isn't prom weekend, and you have time to get my dress."

"That should not be a problem. Maggie is going to give me tentative dates, in an email, tomorrow, so we can go over them. She will change anything that is in conflict."

"Oh, so we will talk about it over the weekend."

"No, we will talk about it tomorrow night."

"So you are going to begin working on reading emails right away?"

"Oh, aren't you the smart one."

"You know… the apple…"

"My mother warned me about this day."

They continued eating and talked about Brianna's day. Stephanie had forgotten to tell Brianna about her upcoming plans.

"Oh, by the way, I am going to leave Saturday morning and I won't be back until Sunday night."

"I thought we would talk about the book signing dates?"

"This isn't a book signing, this is a date."

"Daniel?"

"Yes, we are going to a cabin in the mountains for a little getaway."

Brianna rolled her eyes, "Whatever."

"Did you need me for something this weekend?"

"No, I have plans. I just don't like him."

Stephanie was taken aback, "Why is that, you haven't spent any time with him?"

"Exactly. Don't you think he should want to meet me if he plans to be with you long term?"

Stephanie had not thought about that. "Possibly, but we don't need to rush anything."

"It's been what, nearly a year? I don't call that rushing it."

"Alright, I will talk to him about coming over for dinner one night next week. How does that sound?"

"You can ask him. Let me know and I will invite Josie."

"Josie? Why does he have to meet Josie?"

"I just don't want to be uncomfortable. If I have her here, it won't be weird."

Now it was Stephanie's turn to roll her eyes, "If it makes you happy, she can come over."

Stephanie got up from the table and cleared the dishes. After placing them in the dishwasher, she went upstairs to get out of her clothes. It had been a long day and she needed to relax.

CHAPTER 6

S TEPHANIE GRABBED HER BRIEFCASE, a cup of tea, and headed into the living room. She placed the tea on the end table and sat on the sofa. She grabbed the remote and turned on the tv before sitting back and breaking open her briefcase.

Checking her phone, she saw that Zachary had sent her a message. Before responding, she sent a quick message to Daniel:

Good evening, handsome. What are you up to?

She then read Zachary's:

I hope you are having a good day. Maggie reached out to me today about the tour. It's a great idea and I will work on the dates she forwarded. I will see what I can do about getting product placement as well.

Hmm, she guessed that Maggie had sent the email about the dates. She now knew the first thing she needed to do when she broke open the laptop was to check email.

My day went well. I haven't gotten a chance to check the email yet. I did speak with my daughter and give her a heads up on the plan.

Zachary responded before she had time to open her computer.

Did we discuss how old she was?

Stephanie had to think about that for a minute

I don't know if we did. She is a senior in high school.

Zachary:

Has she chosen a college?

Stephanie:

Not yet. We are beginning to look and make plans for visits.

Zachary:

There are a few stops on the tour with great colleges. Maybe you could multi task the trips and not leave her alone all the time. She might enjoy that.

That thought had not crossed her mind, but it was something to consider. The actual time she would be at a signing would only be a few hours of the day, it might give them time to enjoy the sights. It had been a few years since she and Brianna had gotten the chance to vacation.

I like the way you think. That is a wonderful idea. We have not gone anywhere in such a long time. Even if we didn't visit colleges we could sightsee. Such a smart man. Lol

Zachary:

Yes, I am more than just a pretty face. Lol, I'm going to play poker with the guys, enjoy the rest of your evening!

Stephanie:

Thank you, I will!

Okay, she now knew that the dates had been solidified. She quickly opened up her email from Maggie to see the dates.

Wow, Maggie had outdone herself. She might have been wrong about having time to be a tourist. The calendar was jamb packed with signings. Not surprising, Maggie was always trying to get the biggest bang for the buck. That was great for Stephanie's wallet, but not good for the new idea Zachary had just floated. It would be okay, she hadn't said anything to Brianna, so no one was the wiser.

She began answering other emails and working on a few files. The night progressed quickly. Before she knew it, Brianna was in the kitchen to grab a drink before bed.

Stephanie looked at the time, "I can't believe it's this late. I got the email from Maggie. Do you want to go over it?"

"Just forward the email. You know how to do that, right? I will look it over tomorrow. I'm really tired and I want to go to sleep."

"Haha, smartass. I'll send it to you and we can discuss it over dinner tomorrow night."

"I won't be here for dinner tomorrow night. We are going out for pizza after the football game."

"Oh, okay… when should we talk about it?"

"I'll take a look at it against the school calendar and let you know if there are any conflicts."

"When will you do that?"

"I'll shoot you an email tomorrow when I have a study hall."

Stephanie cocked her head, "Are you serious? You are going to email me?"

"Of course mom, that how things are done these days. Would you prefer a video conference?"

"Go to bed."

Brianna laughed, "Yes, old woman. Good night."

"Good night, smarty pants."

Brianna looked her way and shook her head. You could tell she wasn't impressed with the comeback. Stephanie went back to her work. She finished the file and decided maybe it was time for her to retire as well.

She placed everything in her briefcase and put it on a chair in the kitchen. She glanced at her phone and was surprised to see that she had not missed a message from Daniel. Oh well, they had the weekend to talk. Better to clean everything up now so there would be no interruptions.

She was drying off her face when she heard that sound from her phone. A smile came across her face.

Daniel:

Gorgeous… rest your beautiful tits on my thighs while you enjoy my hard cock before we sleep.

Stephanie climbed into bed before responding:

Certainly. You are very hard tonight. He will taste so good.

Daniel:

Let me get in position to enjoy my fingers in your hair and rub your nipples. I may pump my hips until I can relax. Amazing how enjoyable watching my cock disappear in your throat.

Stephanie placed her hand in her underwear and slid a finger between her lips:

You may pump those hips as you wish. I want you to enjoy.

Daniel:

I like fucking your mouth… but for now I will sit back and watch. I will stand when I am ready to fuck your lovely tits and amazing mouth.

Stephanie continued to circle her clit:

Just relax. You've had a long day. You deserve to release your cum all over me.

Daniel:

I'm ready my sexy slave.

Stephanie:

Let me devour your cock. I'm so hungry for him.

Daniel:

Please do, so hard and thick.

Stephanie:

Sucking him in and out. Moaning with delight.

Daniel:

You moan so nicely.

Stephanie:

I enjoy sucking your cock.

She slid her finger into her wet pussy. She was very aroused and was not waiting until the end of this conversation. A second digit soon joined the first. She began pumping her cunt hard. Her breathing became shallow. She had climbed the mountain and... needed... just... a... moment... more... Yes! There it was, those fabulous orgasmic waves overtaking her entire body. She remained quiet, just little peeps as she finished.

She pulled her fingers from her crotch and gave them a lick as she moved the covers out of the way so she could go to the bathroom and wash up. She washed her hands and returned to her bed to continue her sexting with Daniel.

Daniel:

Vibration of your lips, so nice.

Stephanie:

Letting you know my enjoyment.

Daniel:

Love the pleasure you derive from my cock.

Stephanie:

I could suck him all night.

Daniel:

I would love that. Do you mind sucking him when not fully erect?

Stephanie:
No
Daniel:
Then it could be all night!
Stephanie:
I doubt he would be soft for long.
Daniel:
Well, like a roller coaster, up and down, up and down.
Stephanie:
That will be fun.
Daniel:
How does the head feel?
Stephanie:
So Soft. Very engorged. Love licking his rim.
Daniel:
We love it too!
Stephanie:
He dances so well when I tickle his divot with my tongue.
Daniel:
Fuck... that is amazing.
Stephanie:
He is very responsive.
Daniel:
Very, like your nipple, pinched hard between my fingers.
Stephanie:
My nipples enjoy your touch. They are the ignition that lights the fires within. Are you ready to place your cock between them?
Daniel:
I certainly am. Straddling you, push those tits up and around my manhood. I only want to see your tongue on my tip. Hold them there like a good little girl while I move back and forth.
Stephanie:
He is encased in my breasts. Catching as much of the head as I can as he pokes through the mounds of flesh. Pearl necklace or swallowed?
Daniel:
You know I enjoy the pearls, baby. Just a few more... FUCK... seems

a few pearls found your lips. Lick them off for me.
Stephanie:
I will as I lick your head. Wouldn't want to waste anything.
Daniel:
Absolutely gorgeous. Now roll over and get some sleep. Nighty Night.
Stephanie:
Good night handsome.

Stephanie double checked that she had set her alarm and turned out the light before tucking herself under the covers. She had so many things to prepare for, the most important being her weekend at the cabin with him. One more day, maybe she would be sucking his cock all night long. It certainly was her plan.

CHAPTER 7

FRIDAY WENT BY QUICKLY, and uneventfully. Brianna had messaged her about the tour schedule, no conflicts. Daniel had been quiet, and Zachary did not message her at all. It was now Saturday morning. She was in the kitchen making a breakfast that she would share with Brianna before heading out with Daniel.

Breakfast was almost ready. She turned everything on low and headed toward the stairs. As she reached the bottom and lifted her leg to the first tread, Brianna began bounding down from above.

"Perfect timing. I was just about to come up and get you."

"I could smell everything, and I am starving."

They walked into the kitchen. "Didn't you have pizza last night?"

"I did, but only one slice. By the time I went back for a second, it was gone. I didn't feel like buying a whole pizza just to have another piece."

"Couldn't you have just bought a slice?"

"It's not the same. Plus I wasn't that hungry."

"I see," Stephanie was plating the food. She placed it on the table before continuing. "So what will you do while I'm gone? I picked up a couple of things at the store last night, since I was alone."

"I'm going to drive over to Josie's and we are going to head to the mall. I have to work from four to nine."

"Are you okay coming home to an empty house?"

"Uh, yeah. It's not like I haven't done it before."

"True, but I still wanted to make sure."

"Plus, Mandy might sleep over tonight. It depends if she is

mad at her mom or not."

Mandy was Stephanie's niece. She and Brianna were very close and spent quite a bit of time together. Knowing that Mandy might be over relieved Stephanie's mind.

"That's good. I did pick up popcorn, but if you want soda, you will need to get it before you come home."

"Did you get any pizza?"

"Yes I got pizza. I'm sure the cashier thought I was going on a binge. The only thing missing was massive amounts of wine."

"You could have just gotten us a box."

"Haha. Not happening in my house. And certainly not when I am away."

"Chill. That's not an issue for us and you know it."

"Yes I do."

They continued to chat as they finished their meal. Today Brianna cleared the table and put the dishes in the dishwasher. Stephanie was taken aback. Her baby was growing up. She now believed that these short trips she would soon be making regularly would not be an issue.

Stephanie went up the stairs and into her room to begin packing. He had said not to bring much, but the thought of sitting on that leather couch naked just wasn't appealing. She pulled out three of her sexiest panties with matching bras. She packed two and placed the other set on the bed for later.

She went back into her closet for a nice outfit to wear for dinner. She weeded through her dresses to find just the right one. Ahh, there it was, a sleeveless, burgundy, high necked dress with a peek-a-boo opening that teased her cleavage. The length ended just above her knee. It was form fitting and perfect to combine reserved, yet sexy. She grabbed an off-white shrug with silver flecks to keep out the chill.

All she needed were yoga pants, jeans and a couple of shirts. She would more than likely wear jeans for the ride there and a button front shirt.

She finished placing her clothes in the tiny suitcase and headed into the bathroom to take a shower.

She ran the water and undressed as it warmed. She was very excited for this new chapter. It was exactly what she wanted and yearned for. She opened the shower door and stepped in.

As she rubbed her puff over her body, she touched her nipples with the finger of her other hand. She began to get aroused. She lingered for a short time before coming to her senses. She didn't have time for this now and really had no reason to satisfy herself when he would be doing that for her in just a short time. She continued to cleanse her body and daydream about the rest of her day.

A few minutes later, she exited the shower and dried off. She took a quick look at the time. She still had 25 minutes. He had sent her a text last night that she would picked up at 10:30 this morning. She quickly dressed and put on her face, packing each item when she finished.

She double checked that she had everything she needed. Feeling prepared, and with five minutes to spare, she grabbed her things and went downstairs. She dropped her bag by the front door before walking into the living room to sit and wait.

She decided to check her social media while she waited. She giggled and liked a few cute puppy memes, shared a DIY craft for Brianna. It was now 10:30, but no Daniel. A message alert came in, but it wasn't Daniel, it was Zachary.

How is my successful writer this morning? I am flying home today. Hope you have a wonderful weekend.

Stephanie:

Good morning. I am doing well, just waiting for Daniel. We are spending the weekend together.

Zachary was quite surprised by that text. This was unexpected. Could Daniel really have changed?

That's great! I hope it turns out to be everything you are expecting. Just don't forget about me next week.

Now Stephanie was the one off guard. Did she miss something? As far as she could remember, next week would be her first book signing. She thought it was something local, but could it be in LA? She would have to check.

I'm not following. What do you mean by not forgetting about you? Did we have plans that I forgot?

Zachary:

Lol, no we did not have plans. I just don't want you to get so caught up in him that you forget about me hanging out over here waiting to see you again.

Stephanie:

Whew! I thought I might be losing it. I didn't think I would forget having plans with you.

Zachary:

I will be looking at my schedule when I get back and see when I can meet you on the road. Should I tell you or just let it be a surprise?

Stephanie:

I would prefer to know in case I bring my daughter.

Zachary:

Understandable, I will let you know early in the week. I hope it's soon, I miss that smile.

Stephanie:

Only the smile?

Zachary:

No, also your personality, charm, conversation.

Stephanie:

And…

Zachary:

And what? You mean the sex? Of course that is a welcomed addition, but it's not necessary if you chose to refrain.

Stephanie:

I call bullshit. If that was the case, why was our time together littered with sex?

Zachary:

I don't recall you complaining. It was a fun time, but if your relationship with Daniel changes, I don't want you to think that we can't be together because I will expect sex. That's up to you, I will never force you.

Stephanie:

Thank you. I appreciate your sentiment.

Zachary:

Okay, I've held you up long enough I'm going to say enjoy your weekend. What time are you leaving?

Stephanie looked at the time:

Thirteen minutes ago.

Maybe he had not changed. Zachary:

Well then I really need to let you go. I hope he's waiting in the driveway.

Stephanie:

Thank you! Have a safe trip home!

Zachary:

I will.

Stephanie placed the phone down on her lap. Her excitement was fading. It would be a huge let down if he didn't show. He could have messaged her to say he was running late. Did something happen to him? If it did, how would she know?

She was jolted out of her thought by the doorbell. She wanted to jump out of the chair and run to the door, but she didn't. He could wait a few seconds after letting her sit for nearly 20 minutes. She picked up her bag and opened the door.

"Hello beautiful, are you ready to go?"

"Let me just tell Brianna," she turned to the stairs and yelled up to Brianna. "I'm heading out."

"Okay, I'll see you tomorrow," Brianna yelled back. There was no way Brianna was coming downstairs while Daniel was there, she would not meet him this way.

Stephanie turned back to Daniel, "I guess I am free to go."

"I guess you are," Daniel chuckled. They walked out to the car. Daniel placed her bag in the trunk and opened her door. He kissed her gently as she passed by.

Daniel jogged around the car and sat in the driver's seat. As they pulled out of the driveway, Daniel apologized. "Honey, I'm sorry I was late. I had to get keys made for the office and drop them off to the new guy. We are so busy right now I have them alternating Saturdays. I got a message from him early this morning, but I had to wait for the hardware store to open. I hope the rest of our time together makes up for this."

To her it didn't matter, he was already forgiven. They were on their way to their secret place and she was beyond words.

"This weekend will be wonderful. I thought it would never get here."

"You only needed to wait a few days."

"Not exactly what I meant."

"Huh?"

"Nothing, just thinking out loud."

She was referring to the fact that she wasn't sure she would ever get any extended time with him. Before this week he had never given any inclination that he might be thinking this way. In her mind, this was a major turn in her life. It wasn't something she wanted to discuss with him right now.

"So tell me about the book signings, when do they begin?"

"They start next weekend. Maggie has them set up so I have a break every four weeks. Next weekend is only a couple of hours away, so that won't be bad. We will drive there Saturday afternoon. She has two signings set and then she wants me to make an appearance at a Black and Blue Ball. We will stay at a local hotel and then head a few miles further north for Sunday. I should be home by eight that night. That gives me a little time to spend with Brianna before we head to bed."

"Sounds like Maggie has you pretty busy. I guess sexting will be out of the question."

"It does seem like a tight schedule, but I'm sure you will find some way to take care of yourself while I'm gone."

"I'm sure I can," he took her hand to his lips and kissed it. "But it won't be nearly as good."

A smile came across her face as it softened, "Aww, that is so sweet. You will have to clear your calendar Monday evening to take care of me properly."

"Don't you think you will find someone at the ball to handle that for you?"

"That is not in the plan, and certainly Maggie will make sure that doesn't happen."

"So, if Maggie would have been with you in LA, you would

48

not have been with Zach?"

Stephanie thought about that for a moment, "If she would have been in the meeting, I don't think he would have tried anything. I think it would have been a typical business meeting, probably taken in a different conference room. I can't imagine him taking his banker into that room."

They chuckled. Daniel again took up the conversation, "I guess having Maggie with you will take getting used to. No good stories, no pics with a dick in your mouth, what am I going to do?"

"I'm sure I will still have stories, they will just be different stories and not necessarily about me."

"I guess you are right. They will surely be good for you and your writing, expanding your horizons, so to speak."

"Yes, it will expose me to other areas of the lifestyle. But you know me, I like to watch people and figure out what is in their heads."

"I enjoy watching, but I could give a damn what they are thinking, just put on a good show!"

Stephanie joined his laugh, shaking her head. She was much more cerebral than he was, he was all action. The only thought he had is—what will come next.

"You are such a guy."

"I have never heard you complain about that before. I just remember you saying – yes, more, fuck yes, fuck me harder. It would be tough to follow through if I wasn't such a *guy*."

"Yes, I know, you are very good in that department. I have never complained; other than I might have been sore. But even that was not a complaint, more a glowing endorsement for you."

He laughed hard. "I aim to please. I never get complaints."

"None of your women complain?"

"Now what have I said before, a gentleman doesn't kiss and tell."

She wasn't going to get her answer. Was it because there wasn't anyone else? With as busy as he had been in the office, how could there be? He barely had the time to pull away for her. She decided now was not the time to push the issue. She was going to have a wonderful weekend with him and take things as they came.

"I do enjoy your kisses."

"I think you will get your fill of them this weekend."

"I'm sure I will," she moved in the seat, making herself more comfortable as she stared out the window.

The remainder of the trip was quiet. The only sound was the song on the radio.

CHAPTER 8

A S THEY PULLED INTO THE DRIVEWAY, Stephanie began to feel emotions that she was not quite prepared for. The moment she had been waiting for was now here. She was going to spend the weekend with the love of her life. Her eyes began to well up. She couldn't let him see her cry.

She stared out her window as he parked the car. While he walked around to open her door, she quickly blotted the tears before they spilled down her cheeks. She tried to keep her head down as she got out of the car. As she stood, he placed his hand beneath her chin and lifted her lips to his.

"I hope I live up to those expectations," Daniel said as he pulled away from her.

She cocked her head, "What do you mean?"

"I see those eyes. I hate to make them unhappy."

"I'm not unhappy, just the opposite."

"I know, baby. I just want this to be the memory you have been waiting for."

"You know it will be. It already is."

Daniel grabbed their bags from the trunk before they walked toward the cabin.

"Do you have your key? My hands are a bit full."

Stephanie pulled out her keychain and unlocked the door. Daniel pushed it open for her to walk through. They entered the cabin. Daniel dropped the bags and pulled Stephanie close. He began pecking her gently on the lips, his hands on her back.

His kisses became stronger, his hand wandered to her ass. He grabbed a handful of her bum as he passionately drove his tongue deep into her mouth, exploring every centimeter. She was panting, small moans were beginning to escape.

He placed his hands on her shoulders and tenderly pushed her away.

"Let me take our bags into the bedroom. Have a seat on the sofa."

She pouted a bit. He raised his eyebrows and gave a little turn to his head. She turned and walked to the couch. He bent down and picked up the bags to take into the bedroom.

He seemed to be lingering in the bedroom. How long could it possibly take to throw bags on the bed? A couple of minutes later, he walked into the kitchen area, grabbed glasses out of the cabinet and poured them each a glass of orange juice. He brought them over to her.

"We will start with this, you need your energy."

"What do you have planned?"

"Well, I was thinking we could have sex, then we could go outside and fuck. Followed by lunch, and a blow job. Eventually we will need to go out and grab a bite to eat. When we get back, we could make out as our food digests and then head back to the bedroom for the all night suckfest you tell me you would like to do."

She showed confusion in her straight face as he expressed his thoughts for the weekend.

"Hmm, that is so not what I was thinking. I was expecting talking, then a bit of debate. I imagined us discussing our childhood, expressing our view on the universe and some cuddling before drifting off into a snuggling sleep session."

She could only hold her position for a moment after the words were out before she began laughing. She leaned toward him and kissed his lips.

"I know why we are here, and I love the idea of spending the weekend naked with you, examining every inch of this cabin for ways to christen every speck of our love shack."

"I'm glad we are both on the same page."

They sipped the juice as he rubbed his hand on her leg. There was no reason for words; their actions would speak for them.

He slowly stroked her thigh and then lifted her leg onto his lap. His fingers continued up and down her calf. When he got to her foot, he pushed off her shoe, its thud being the only noise.

Realizing the quiet, Daniel picked up the remote from the coffee table and turned on some soft music. His movements were in perfect sync with the rhythm. He moved from under her leg and took her glass, placing it on the table. He pushed her limb toward the back of the cushion. He slid off her other shoe and got on his knees between her thighs. He began kissing her and nudging her to lay back.

Her hands ran through his thick hair. They continued to kiss as his body came to rest on hers. Feeling him on her was a welcomed sensation. She longed to have this intimacy. This was the closest they had ever come to making love. She wanted desperately to make that connection.

He rubbed her breast. Her nipples were hard. His hand found its way under her top and pushed toward the goal. Finding her bra, he pulled the tit from its holster and uncovered the mound. His tongue encircled the peak before his teeth bit softly on the protruding flesh.

She wiggled a bit in enjoyment, her hand still in his mane. His other hand followed the first. He pressed her bosom together and began nibbling on both nipples. Her hips began to gyrate. Her knees pulled up his sides. Her body wanted him.

He crawled away from her boobs. His hands loosened her pants. He grabbed the waist and began to pull as she lifted her rear from the sofa. He pulled the panties off with her jeans, throwing them on the floor. He crossed his arms and grabbed the bottom of his shirt, lifting it over his head and throwing it across the room.

He placed his hands on her lips and parted them. He rubbed his thumb across her glistening clit. It was engorged. He bent over and began licking, then sucking her hooded friend. He began slow and soft. He unceasingly increased his intensity until her hips were writhing and she was screaming lustfully.

He knew she had climbed the mountain and needed to cross the precipice. Using two fingers on his right hand, he drove them into her pussy and circled her g-spot.

She began screaming, lifting her head, and digging her nails into the couch. He continued stimulating her into multiple orgasms. He wanted her to squirt before he would cease. She fought releasing her juices.

"Let it go, baby. I want to watch you spray."

She knew she couldn't fight him. He wasn't stopping. She was in overload. She stopped fighting and began flowing. He began pumping her cunt even harder as the fluid splashed through the air. She could feel the droplets all over her body. She screamed and arched her back.

Feeling that she had fully released, Daniel slowed and stopped. He pulled his fingers from her sopping hole and stuck them in her mouth. She cleaned them for him.

He stood and walked into the bathroom, returning with a towel. He wiped the leather and wedged it under her behind.

Her eyes were glazed as she looked at him. He unbuckled his belt, unbuttoned and unzipped his pants, dropping them to the ground. He sat and took off his shoes before pulling his legs from his trousers. He pushed himself back on the sectional and spread his legs. She knew that was her invitation to return the benefit.

She knelt in front of him. She was hungry for his cock. It was standing tall, awaiting the warm confines behind her lips. She wasted no time, taking the head directly in. She began moving his manhood in and out of her mouth, going further down his shaft with each stroke.

You could hear the delight in her soft moans, adding to the sensations on his dick. He rested his head atop the couch. He basked in the excitement of her task. Her hand began cupping his balls. The suction became more passionate. He could feel her finger wandering behind his balls and toward his puckered hole.

He lifted his head, placed his hand under her chin, and pulled her face to his.

"Not yet," he whispered as he kissed her lips. "You are such good girl, but it's not time for your reward."

There was a bit of sadness that crossed her face. He smiled and gave her a hug.

"I don't want to waste something now, that I might need a little later. I'm not a spring chicken."

They both chuckled. She knew she had not done anything wrong and had much more in store for later.

"Sit down a second, I'll be right back."

Daniel hopped up and walked to the bedroom. He quickly returned with matching robes.

"Get rid of your shirt and bra, then put this on."

She did as she was told. Daniel threw on his robe and grabbed the glasses to refill. When he returned, he sat next to her again.

"I think you might need this."

"I think I do. I was getting a little light headed. You just would not let up."

"I wanted what I wanted, and you were not giving it to me. You should know better, I always get what I want."

It was true, he always did.

CHAPTER 9

THEY TOOK A LITTLE TIME to catch up on their weeks, commiserating over things that did not go well, and chuckling over the craziness that just spontaneously happens. When Daniel felt they had caught up on everything, he stood, took her glass, and headed to the kitchen to make lunch.

"I hope you don't mind, but I just threw together some turkey salad. I also went by the Italian bakery and grabbed the coleslaw you like. I'll make it up to you tomorrow, steaks on the grill."

From her seat on the sofa she replied, "Don't worry about it. We can't eat too heavy if you want to get in all the sex you have on the agenda."

They laughed. She enjoyed seeing him like this. The side she saw was very different than the one he presented to the business world. In that world he was stodgy and stoic. Never a hair out of place, clothes perfectly pressed, impeccably dressed. He would smile politely, but never a good belly laugh. Always the professional.

She wanted to see him open up a little more in those situations. She knew he was concerned that people would not take him seriously if he did, but she knew he was so wrong. People in their circles knew there was a little devil in him, they just never witnessed it.

She wondered if things would change when he retired and had no reason to impress colleagues any longer. She was excited for the day when he would just let his hair down and enjoy all of life. Right now she would just have to accept his old school attitudes and pray for a lighter soul in the future.

He was almost finished putting together the sandwiches.

She wandered over to the island, pulled out a chair, and sat down.

He reached across the island to place their plates. "Would you prefer iced tea or wine with your lunch?"

"Iced tea, I'll need the caffeine to keep up with you."

"Baby, you never have any problems in that area."

"Thank you, handsome. You certainly keep me on my toes."

"Only when I need your pussy a little higher to stick my dick into her."

"That's what they make stilettos for."

He kissed her on the cheek as he took his seat next to her. "I love your silliness."

Well at least he loves something, now if he would just admit to loving the whole package, she would be set. She would not pressure him. She wasn't going anywhere, and neither was he. They both had the perfect relationship, why complicate things?

"The turkey salad is delicious. I'm quite impressed with your skills."

"My mother was a great cook and since she didn't have a daughter, we were her replacements. Anything she would have taught a daughter, she taught her boys. It did come in handy in college. I had been known to help my wife, at the time, with dinner prep and chores. I have to admit I didn't cook often because I was better than she was, and I didn't want to hurt her feelings."

"Well, I will never stop you from cooking for me. Suzie Homemaker I am not. It's not that I can't cook, it's that I really don't like to." She thought for a moment, then added, "Scratch that. I do love to have dinner parties and try new recipes to impress guests. It's just that with it only being Brianna and myself, it's not much fun. Soon it will be just me. At that point I won't even need a stove. Take out or microwave for me."

"That's right, you will be an empty nester. I'll be able to stop by anytime and ravage you anywhere in the house. That will be lots of fun." He leaned over and placed a peck on her cheek.

She became warm inside. He was talking about the future

and she was in it. This really was moving in the direction she had been hoping for all this time. She felt like her heart would burst out of her chest. There was nothing more she could want; she was truly satisfied.

Daniel took the plates over to the sink. He refilled their drinks before making an odd suggestion.

"Let's go for a short walk."

"Okay, I'll get dressed."

"No. You don't need to get dressed. It's not that cold. Let's just go out in our robes. Just grab your shoes."

This was unexpected. The sun was shining, but they were in the woods. There had been a chill in the air when they arrived. She got up from the island and slid on her shoes. Daniel had already put on some moccasins.

He took her by the hand and led her out the door. There was a trail off the back of the deck. He led the way, making sure she was watching her step.

They walked a short distance through the brush until they came to a clearing. There was a beautiful, clear lake. A set of stairs led down a bank to the dock. At the top of the stairs was a large boulder. They sat on its flat surface.

"This is gorgeous. I would never have expected to be this close to the lake."

"It is a plus. I have a small boat that I put in the lake during the summer. Imagine sex in the middle of the lake."

"During the day or evening?"

"Daytime of course."

"Wouldn't there be other people on the lake?"

"At times there are."

"You are such a showoff."

"Hey, I would let them join. If it was okay with you."

"Seems I have heard that before."

"I've learned to share my toys."

Stephanie felt like she had taken a step back. Was she really just a toy? It must have been something he let slip, he certainly was not acting that way this weekend. She would not dwell on it; she wanted to enjoy the moment.

He put his arm around her. Her thoughts cleared as she snuggled into him. She put her arms around him and held him tight. As she nuzzled his neck, she placed a few small kisses.

He put his other arm around her and pulled her close. He placed his lips on her forehead. She was in heaven, nothing could be more perfect.

He moved his hand to her chin and lifted her lips to his. He looked into her eyes as they kissed softly. Her eyes were smiling. His hand moved down to her waist and began loosening the sash on her robe. Her lips became tighter as she smiled, he was such a stinker.

He pushed her robe off her shoulder and down her arm. He cupped her breast, rubbing his thumb over her wrinkled areola and stiff nipple. Was she extremely horny or just cold? He was about to find out.

He pulled his mouth from hers and stood in front of her. The sun was shining brightly on her skin, but there was not enough of it showing. He pushed the rest of the garment from her body, laying it out behind her.

Without a word, he gently nudged her body onto the rock. He spread her legs and opened the front of his robe. His cock was erect. He slid the head up and down her slit, making sure she was moist before pushing into her cunt.

He went slowly, going deeper with each stroke. He continued with a slow pace, not wanting to cause any pain on the hard surface.

She enjoyed every plunge of his rod. Suddenly she was startled out of her trance by a snapping of a branch and the crunch of leaves. Her head lifted.

"What was that?"

"I'm sure it was nothing, maybe a rabbit."

"That seemed a bit loud for a rabbit."

The sound of someone, or something, stepping on leaves and breaking twigs continued and was moving closer. Fear crossed her face. She was not willing to be seen by animal, or man. She pulled her pussy away from him and began scrambling to get her robe on.

She was nearly covered when two men came out of the woods carrying fishing rods and tackle. They looked as surprised as Stephanie.

"Oh my, we are so sorry for interrupting."

Stephanie closed her robe and tied the sash. She was looking down at her feet, not wanting to look the men in the eyes. Daniel was quite the opposite. He nonchalantly moved his cock back behind his robe and began to talk to them.

"Not to worry. We have all weekend. I would have continued, but someone is a bit more shy."

He placed his arm around her shoulder.

"We don't usually run into anyone out here this time of year. Most of the cabins are only used in the summer and during the ski season."

"No need to explain. No harm was done and now you have a really good fishing story."

They all laughed. The men wished them a good day and continued down the stairs and to the dock.

Stephanie's heart was beating out of her chest. Daniel hugged her.

"Honey, don't worry, they will never say a word. Even if they did, no one would believe them. Would you like a glass of wine now?"

"I might need your Jack and Coke."

They laughed, and he led her back to the cabin.

CHAPTER 10

THEY ENTERED THE CABIN and walked into the kitchen.

"Did you really want the Jack?"

"No, that's fine. I would have liked to crawl under a rock. It never crossed my mind that there could be other people around. I realize that your cabin isn't the only one up here, but I did think that was your dock."

"There are a few docks around the lake and everyone shares them. There might be six other cabins that use the one I do."

"Oh great, so there could have been a parade of people wandering through. I guess we are lucky it was only two guys. Have you ever met them before?"

"I might have seen them once or twice when I brought the boat in. They seem to be avid fishers. I doubt they catch anything."

"Well they caught an eyeful today! They saw at least one breast, possibly some action. Was this the first time they caught you?"

"Now, now, you know a gentleman never kisses and tells."

"They didn't catch you kissing."

He handed her a glass of wine. "I am always the gentleman."

In other words, he was not going to tell her how many other women he had taken out to the boulder. She took a sip of her wine and pondered that thought. Had there been a steady stream of women, or was she the only one? She wanted to believe it was just her, but how could she know for sure? Were his boasts of other women just his way of making up for his jealousy over her other men? Did he forget the other men were his idea? Today she was the only one; that was enough for her.

"What are you thinking?" he asked her.

"I'm thinking how lucky I am to be here with you. I'm the luckiest woman in the world."

"I think I am the lucky one. There are so many others that you could be with."

"But I only want to be with you."

"I doubt that. You get tons of attention everywhere you go."

"So? You get attention as well; does that mean you want to fuck all of them?"

"No, only the good looking ones," he laughed, but she was not seeing the humor. Was he serious? "Baby, relax, don't look so concerned, I was just kidding."

Of course he was, why would he want anyone else when he had someone who by all rights was perfect? She was attractive, smart, funny, charismatic, self-confident, and great in bed. She was also completely dedicated to him, what more could he want?

"Sometimes I wonder…"

"Wonder about what?!? You know how much I care about you. You are the one I trust the most. I care about you more than any of the others."

She lifted an eyebrow, "Any of the others?"

"You know what I mean. We are free to date other people."

Her heart sank again. How many others were there? Why wouldn't he admit to them? Why the secrets? Were they really there or was this his dominant talk again? She didn't know what to believe. She had no proof of anyone else. Without proof to convince her otherwise, her mind decided this was just talk and his fear of committal.

She walked over to him and gave him a hug. "You're right. Whatever you want."

"I want to sit on the sofa with you and catch a little golf."

She pulled back, "Seriously?"

"Yes. There is a big tournament this weekend. I just want to see who the leaders are, we need to recoup anyway."

"Speak for yourself, I'm ready to go."

"Oh really? My cock is always between my legs when you

want to suck it."

"I know where your cock is. I'll sit with you and drink my wine. Who knows what will happen."

She turned toward the couch. He walked behind her with his hand on the small of her back. She placed her glass on the coffee table before she sat and waited for him to get comfortable. She watched him organize his remotes and drink. When he was settled she snuggled into his chest.

Daniel picked up the remote and turned on his golf tournament. She tucked her legs onto the sofa. His arm was around her. She had one arm on his hip and the other around his stomach. As she wedged herself against him, she began rubbing her hand through the hair on his chest.

◆

"Oh fuck!" Daniel exclaimed, waking Stephanie. She sat up next to him. "Sorry baby, it was such a close game. I didn't mean to wake you. Did you have a nice nap?"

"Yes I did," she said as she stretched. "I didn't realize I was tired. What would have happened if I drank my wine?"

"I would have found a way to wake you."

She took her glass off the table and took a sip. It was warmer than she liked. She stood to get a few ice cubes. "Do you need another drink?"

"You don't have to do that, I can get it."

"It's my turn." She took his glass and went into the kitchen.

She put a few cubes in her glass and refreshed his, before returning to the couch. She was smiling as she handed him the glass.

"What's on your mind?" Daniel said with a sly tone.

"Nothing, why do you ask?"

"You have this devious little smile on your pretty face. I'm wondering if I should be worried."

"You, be worried? No, that's not an issue."

"Well that's good. There's just a little more of this round.

When it's over we can get ready for dinner."

"Okay," she snuggled into him. As she drank her wine, she thought about the dream she had during her short rest.

She was in a long white dress, bouquet in her hand, waiting in a small room. A man walked up to her, took her hand and led her out a door and onto a beach. There were guests and a man holding a book under an arch facing them. She had awoken before walking down the aisle. She also found it strange that she had not seen the man's face. Certainly, since she was asleep in Daniel's arms, it had to be a premonition about them. That thought warmed her body. She snuggled a little tighter.

"Honey, I don't think you can get any closer."

"I'm not sure about that. I'll keep trying."

They giggled, and she sipped her wine quietly, waiting for the round to be over.

Before her glass was empty, the round was finished. Daniel turned the TV off and stood up, putting his hand out to her.

"Shall we Miss?"

"Sure."

They walked toward the bedroom.

"Why don't you hop in the shower first, I want to quickly check emails and see if there are any fires to be put out."

She kissed him and headed into the bathroom. She opened the shower door, started the water, and checked to see if everything she needed was in the shower. There was no conditioner. She walked back into the bedroom to grab hers from the luggage.

Daniel was sitting in a chair with his phone, there was a shitty grin on his face. When he realized she was in the room, he placed his phone on his chest.

"What do you need baby?"

"There wasn't any conditioner in the shower. I'll just get mine really quick."

"Do you need anything else?"

"I don't think so. You have everything well stocked."

"Whatever you need, just holler and I'll get it."

"Okay," she walked over and gave him a kiss.

Back in the bathroom, she began undressing. This was very odd. He typically went into the shower with her when she had showered at his house. He was an expert on close-quarter positions. What was going on today?

She stood under the steady stream of water, thinking as she washed her body. Something didn't feel right, but she shrugged it off considering they had so much time together and there was no need to constantly be all over each other.

She rinsed her hair and lingered under the warm water. It felt so relaxing. She turned and let it rain down on her face. The shower cleansed her soul as well as her body.

She stood there for a few minutes before turning off the water. She could have stood there forever, but Daniel still needed a shower and she was sure he would want hot water.

She opened the door and grabbed her towel from the warmer. She began to pat off before stepping out, wrapping herself in the fluffy cloth. She walked over to the mirror and ran her fingers through her hair.

She turned to walk into the bedroom as Daniel walked in. He had removed his pants and was opening his shirt. He stood behind her, placing his arms around her and began kissing her neck. He pressed against her. She could feel his hard cock on her buttocks. She turned and faced him, placing her arms around neck and kissing him with vigor.

The tongue dance continued until she was breathing heavily. Then he pulled back and said, "Alright sexy, I need to get in the shower and you need to finish getting ready. We have reservations."

She pouted and let him go. He gave her a quick peck before turning toward the shower. She went into the bedroom and grabbed her outfit. His phone was vibrating on the chair.

She put on her under garments and slid into her dress. The phone was still vibrating. She grabbed her makeup case and went into the bathroom.

"Your phone is vibrating off the hook. Someone really wants

your attention."

"It's just one of my new guys. I told him who to contact, but I guess he isn't listening."

"Maybe you need to tell him that you are on a sexcapade and don't want to be bothered."

"I think I'll let that tidbit of information out of the conversation."

"You don't think he knows you have sex?"

"No, I'm not saying that. I'm saying he doesn't need to know when I do."

"Ahh, I see."

He turned off the shower and grabbed his towel. She looked at him in the mirror. She turned to him with a look of horror on her face.

"What's wrong!" he exclaimed.

"You're cock," she said pointing to it. "It's not hard. Are you ill? Do you have a fever?"

She walked over to him and put her hand on his forehead.

"Haha, it doesn't need to be hard all the time."

"It should be when I'm around."

"Twenty or thirty years ago that would have been true, not so much anymore."

"That's unfortunate. Could you imagine what would have happencd had we met then?"

"I probably would not have the business I have today. I would have been too distracted."

"Hmm, maybe, or we could have used sex as the carrot for all your hard work."

"Bullshit, we would have had sex no matter what I did or didn't get done."

"Yeah, you're probably right. Things happen when they are supposed to happen, and not a moment sooner."

He kissed her on the cheek, "You are correct, gorgeous."

He went into the bedroom to dress as she finished her makeup. For a moment her mind thought about what would have happened had they met thirty years ago. It would be blissful to think that they could have spent all this time madly in love and enjoy each other, but they weren't the people they are now. She needed to go through the pain and discouragement in order to be the person that stood looking back at her in the mirror today.

Would she have loved the idea of living the fairytale she created in her mind? Certainly, but it was just that, a fairytale. She could hope that one day her life vaguely resembled her thoughts, but only time would tell if that would be the case. For now, things were looking as though they were headed in that direction, and that was all she needed. Her heart was filled. She was feeling emotions she had not experienced before, and for the first time in her life, she was truly happy.

Daniel walked up behind her dressed handsomely, looking like a model that just stepped out of the pages of GQ.

"Almost finished?" he asked.

"Just another minute."

"Okay, I'll have a drink while I wait."

"I'm serious! It will just be a minute. I only need to put on mascara and I'm finished."

"If you say so."

"I say I'm finished. Now where is that white horse?"

He put his arms around her. "Thank you, baby, but I am far from a prince."

"Depends who you ask. To me you are."

He kissed her on the forehead, "You are so sweet."

"Thank you, handsome. Is this dress okay for where we are headed?"

"Yes it is. Although, I would like to see more leg and cleavage."

"You get to see that all the time, I don't want others getting the same view."

"Why not?"

"Imagination, it's a better tease."

"You might be right."

"I know I am," she said as she turned to leave the room. He

spanked her rear. She stopped and turned, "You did say we had reservations? Do you really want to start things now?"

He laughed and swatted her ass again. Oh, how her silliness lightened his mind.

She had laid a shrug on the bed. She went to pick it up, but was told, "I've got this."

Daniel placed the wrap on her shoulders and they headed for the door. He helped her into the car, then they were on their way.

CHAPTER 11

I T WAS JUST A SHORT DRIVE to the restaurant. It was absolutely stunning. A converted 19th century hotel, updated just enough to still give homage to the era of days gone by. The double front doors were adorned with the original leaded glass inserts. The floors were rich with the character of all the travelers who rested their weary heads, up the extra wide stairway, behind the solid wood doors with glass handles.

Stephanie was in awe of the natural beauty that remained, although walls had been refinished with more modern products. It was intoxication for the eyes.

The hostess led them to a table toward the back of the dining room, next to a window. They sat across from each other, in the tufted chairs, smiling in the candlelight.

Stephanie glanced out the window to see a covered porch with a lit walk in the distance. "I wonder where the walk leads?"

"Down to the lake you saw earlier today. You can see it well from here during the day, or on moonlit nights."

"So you come here often?"

"No, sexy, for years this was the only place to eat when we were up here. Since I was the only one of the guys who cooked, we came here often."

"Well, since you have been here so often, you can tell me the best option for dinner."

"I can tell you that I never had anything here that was not amazing. Whatever you are in the mood for, order it and you will have no regrets."

With that the waiter came to the table. "Welcome, can I start you off with a libation?"

"Yes, the lady will have a Moscato, and I will have a Jack and

Coke."

"Before I get your drinks, tonight the soups are lobster bisque and a tomato vegetable. The chef has also made a special meal this evening, chicken rondo, which is a deep-fried quarter with chef's own special sauce, served with your choice of sides."

"Sounds delicious. We will think it over."

The waiter nodded, turned, and headed for the bar. The couple sat quietly looking over their menus. Stephanie placed her bill of fare on the table, having made her decision.

Daniel glanced over his listing. "You've decided? What are you having?"

"Crab cakes with coleslaw."

"Hmm, while that sounds good, I think I'm leaning toward a filet. I need my protein for later."

"Yes you do. Maybe you should order two," she said slyly.

The waiter returned with their drinks. He placed them on the table while asking if they had decided. They each gave their choice. The waiter took their menus, thanked them, and headed to the kitchen.

Daniel placed his hand on the table with his palm up waiting for hers. She eagerly placed it in his. They were quiet for a moment as they stared into each other's eyes.

"You look beautiful tonight, honey. I'm glad you are here with me."

"Thank you, handsome. There is nowhere else I would rather be right now."

She began rubbing his calf with her foot. She wanted to kiss him, but they were not close enough. She looked at him with a sultry stare. Her heart could not get more full. A weekend with the love of her life, a romantic dinner, she could only imagine what the rest of the night could hold.

"What are you thinking about, baby?" Daniel asked.

"I'm thinking how lucky I am right now. We are alone, at a very romantic restaurant, and I am going to spend the night with you. What more could I possibly want?"

"Maybe a Maserati?"

"I thought I would wait until my birthday or Christmas to ask for that."

They giggled. The waiter brought a bread basket to the table and refreshed their drinks.

They flirted and talked through dinner. They did not notice any other patrons. For them, they were alone in their own little world. The outside did not matter, it was just the two of them now, the world would have to wait.

They had lingered over their meal. The waiter checked in occasionally. When he asked about dessert, they both declined. Having too much food would deter the plans for the evening. They did decide to have coffee.

When the waiter returned with the receipt, Daniel placed it in his pocket, stood and placed his hand out for Stephanie. She took it and stood. They thanked the waiter and said goodbye to the hostess on the way out the door.

Daniel did not go down the stairs. Instead, he walked Stephanie around the porch to the walkway. They took a romantic stroll down to the lake. The clouds had cleared and the sliver of the moon cast a romantic glow on the lake. Stephanie could imagine how lovely this must be on a clear, full moon.

He held her from behind as they stared at the lake. He turned her toward him and kissed her in the moonlight. She could not imagine anything more romantic. She put her head on his chest and held him tight.

They stayed there a few moments before he pulled back. He gave her a quick kiss on the lips and took her hand to head back to the car.

They passed other guests as they strolled, giving them a polite hello and head nod.

Daniel helped Stephanie into the car before getting in himself, and started the car. He gave her a kiss on the cheek before placing the car in reverse and pulling out of the space. He left the lot and headed back to the cabin.

It was a quiet ride, soft music in the background and more hand holding. This weekend more than met her expectations, and it was far from over. Her heart was soaring, her curiosity piqued. What was in store next?

They arrived back at the cabin. He led her into the bedroom. He took her shrug and placed it on the chair. He was looking at her as he ran his fingers through her hair. He pulled her close and kissed her gently. She wrapped her arms around his chest.

Lips still locked, he began sliding her zipper toward her waist. He grabbed a handful of her full ass, pressing her toward his body. She could feel his arousal.

He put his hands on her shoulders and carefully pushed her away. Taking the fabric on her shoulders and pushing it down her arms, he exposed her lacey black bra. Her nipples shown through the light fabric, he ran his fingers over them lightly. Her slight gasp let him know he was hitting the right spot.

He took off his coat and threw it on the chair. He unbuttoned his shirt and opened it, exposing his skin. He pulled her against him, rubbing his chest with hers. He was watching her face as she closed her eyes and enjoyed the feeling. He reached behind her and unhooked her bra, pulling the straps down and letting it fall to the floor. Skin to skin, he continued.

He hooked his thumbs inside her dress, pushed it past her buttocks, and onto the floor, exposing a black thong. His fingers moved it to the side as he slid one between her lips. She was moist. She opened her legs to give him more access.

His middle finger rubbed and circled her clit with vigor. Her breathing became quicker. He manipulated her clit faster as she became more excited. He was unrelenting. She grabbed his shoulders to steady herself.

She was moaning louder. She was close; he was going to take her over the top. He continued to exploit her engorged clitoris, rubbing and circling. Relentless and determined he continued until that all too familiar scream released from deep inside her body.

Her head was back, her legs were shaking. He slowed, but did not stop until he was sure she had gotten everything out of the orgasm.

She brought her head forward, looking at him with glazed over eyes. She leaned into him until she steadied herself. He put his arms around her.

"Step out of your dress, baby, and lay on the bed."

She did as she was told. She lay on her back across the bed expecting him to place his cock inside her.

He pulled her thong off and removed her shoes. She elevated her head by getting on her elbows so she could watch as he undressed.

He dropped his shirt to the floor. He took off his belt, folded it in half and ran the loop over her nipples, then tapped them lightly a few times. Her hips began heaving. A "no not yet" smirk came over his face as he dropped the strap to the floor.

He loosened his pants and they too joined the other garments on the carpet. He placed his hand in his underwear and pulled out his cock and balls.

"Do you want this, baby?"

"You know I do."

"Where do you want it?"

"I want it everywhere."

"Where should we start?"

"I want to suck him." She began to turn in the bed, bringing her head to the edge.

He pushed down his boxer briefs. She was now in position, head hanging over the bed. He took off his shoes and socks, then teased his cock against her cheeks. She tried to move her lips toward it, but he pulled away.

He grabbed the sides of her face, her mouth was open. He placed the head in, as she began to close around it, he pulled it out. She pouted. Again she opened; again he indulged her, this time pushing as deep as he could. His balls were resting on her nose. He held it there until he felt her begin to gag.

Now that he had proved his dominance, he began fucking her mouth at a steady pace. She was moaning, her hips were writhing, her hands held onto his hips. He pushed deep into her throat, held a moment, then pulled out completely.

"Get out of bed and bend over."

She did as she was ordered.

"Spread your ass."

She placed her head on the bed and put a hand on each cheek. She pulled them apart, giving him access to whichever hole he chose.

"Spread your legs further."

As she did, he began rubbing the tip of his dick the full length of her crack. She began pumping her hips. She was beyond ready.

Knowing he had teased her enough, he lined up with her pussy and pushed his way in.

She could feel every inch of him as he stuffed her full. Her cunt was sopping, no need to stop until her ass was against his groin. He grabbed a handful of hair, pulled her head up, and began riding her like a wild bull.

His balls bounced against her clit, adding to her stimulation. He moved his hands to her hips and drove even harder. Her orgasms were coming in waves. He continued faster. She was screaming, then a primal groan emerged and her juices began to flow. They were running down her legs and dripping from his balls.

He began to slow the pace. Knowing he had satisfied her, he took his cock from her. She was panting.

"Kneel on the floor."

She knew where this was headed. She knelt on the floor in front of him. He stood above her and continued rubbing his shaft.

"Are you ready?'

She shook her head, yes.

"Open your mouth and stick out your tongue. Hold my cum until I tell you to swallow."

She tilted her head a little, closed her eyes, opened her mouth, placed her hands on her thighs, and waited for the warm jizz to spurt from him. She was not waiting long before she felt the warmth land on her face. He brought his tip to her tongue as he squeezed out the last drops.

She opened her eyes and waited for his command.

"You look even more gorgeous this way. You may swallow." He put his hand out to help her off the floor. "Go get yourself washed up. I'll join you in a minute."

She headed to the bathroom. She was covered in cum. Hopping in the shower to rinse off would probably be best. She ran the water, giving it time to warm up, before jumping in and rinsing off. She was exiting the shower as Daniel came in.

"I didn't think I came that much."

"Between your juices and mine, I needed more than a washrag."

He grabbed a rag and ran it under the water. "I have something on the bed for you."

She dried off and went to see what it was. There, lying on the bed, was a deep purple satin negligee. There were matching slippers on the floor. She slid into the outfit just as Daniel walked into the room.

"That looks better than I thought it would."

"You did well. I love the color."

"I was looking for something different. Anyone can have a black, red, or white one."

She walked up to him and gave him a kiss, "Thank you, handsome."

"You're more than welcome, sexy. Give me a second to throw something on and we will go have a drink."

CHAPTER 12

S HE FOLLOWED HIM into the kitchen. She was surprised when he pulled out a small pot and placed it on the stove. He took milk out of the refrigerator and a container of hot chocolate out of the cabinet. What a great idea!

They joked and giggled as the milk warmed. She took over stirring the pot as he placed the mix in the cups. He reclaimed the container as the liquid started a rolling boil. He poured the milk into the mugs, placing the vessel in the sink. He grabbed spoons and used one to stir. He opened another cabinet and took out marshmallow fluff, topped each drink, and left the spoon in his.

They walked over and sat on the couch. They faced each other. Stephanie pulled her legs onto the seat. Her hands were wrapped around the mug.

"This was a great idea. I like the marshmallow on top."

"It's the way my mom always made it. We didn't do it often, only for special occasions."

Only for special occasions? Then this must be one. Her eyes sparkled with happiness.

"You certainly were a momma's boy. I'm okay with that, she did a fabulous job, you cook, you clean, you work; you make the perfect wife!"

The both laughed.

"No, sexy, I would not be the perfect wife, I love sex!"

Stephanie nearly choked on her hot chocolate. "Ah, yes, I forgot about that part. But you could be the truly rare unicorn wife that does it all. How are you with fixing toilets?"

"I'm fabulous! I call the plumber."

"And, you have a wonderful sense of humor. You seem to

have it all."

"Sexy, I am far from the catch you seem to think I am."

She looked into his eyes, what secrets was he keeping? What pain was he hiding? Why would he not open up to her? She wanted those answers, but now was not the time to probe, just enjoy the moment. This was a long time coming and she wanted it to happen again, she couldn't blow it now.

He could see the wheels turning in her mind. He placed his hand on her leg and shook it. "So, are you ready for this next big step in your career? I think it sounds very exciting."

"It's exciting, but a little scary."

"What is scary?"

"What if we put all of this together and no one shows up? What if it's a big flop?"

"I can't believe that you would be so negative."

"I don't see it as negative, I see it as realistic."

"Do you trust Maggie?"

"Of course I do."

"Isn't it her job to make sure people show up?"

"Yes."

"Then why would you think that she would not do her job?"

"It's not that I don't think she will do her job. I just know how people are—they don't always do what they say they will."

"Can you do something for me?"

She thought about that for a minute, "Depends what it is…"

"I want you to only think positive thoughts. I want you to think that there will be lines of people waiting to see you."

She smiled, "I can do that."

"Good."

They continued talking until their cups were empty. They covered her trips, her daughter, colleges; anything that came to mind.

Daniel took their mugs and placed them in the sink with the pot, filling them with water.

He came back to her, took her ankles and straightened her legs. She turned on the sofa. He placed his hands on the back of the couch and leaned in to kiss her gently. He began at the top of her head and worked his way slowly to her lips.

She placed her hands on his waist. He took one hand and slid it down her arm to her hand as he straightened. He took her hand and began to turn. She stood and followed him to the bedroom.

He walked her to the bed before taking her in his arms, caressing her body as their lips mingled. It was slow and very sexy. He was taking his time. As his hands meandered to her bum, he grabbed the fabric and pulled it up and over her head.

He fondled her bare breasts before moving her into bed. He pulled down the covers and placed her on her back. He took off his clothes and left them in a pile on the floor. He climbed in and on top of her. She felt his hard penis against her pelvis.

He kissed her neck and nibbled her ear. He rubbed his chest against hers. He looked into her eyes as he slid his manhood into her awaiting vagina.

His strokes were slow and deliberate. He continued to stare into her eyes. Her orgasms came, but they were different. He watched as her face told him all her secrets. She was in love with him, deeply and madly in love.

Her mind was racing. This was so much different than their normal sex. This time he was not fucking her, he was making love to her. She had her hands in his hair, pulling him close and kissing him deeply.

Their tongues continued to dance until he was ready to cum. He straightened his arms, thrust his cock deep into her, pulled his head back, and moaned low and deep. When he finished, he lowered himself onto her; she held him tight.

They became one for a few minutes. Lifting himself from her, he grabbed tissues from the nightstand and wiped his juice from between her thighs. He grabbed more and cleaned himself.

He laid on his right side and looked lovingly at her.

She looked at him, "Thank you, baby."

He smiled at her, "Roll on your side so I can hold you as I drift off."

She turned away from him. He drew close to her, putting his arm around her. They cuddled until he fell asleep.

It took her a little longer to submit to slumber. She needed to process what had just happened. This was huge. He made love to her. This had elevated their relationship to another level. She was falling deeper into the abyss.

CHAPTER 13

I T WAS STILL DARK when her eyes opened. She was confused, nothing looked familiar. She felt his warm body behind hers. That's right, she was at the cabin and her man was still holding her close.

She lay next to him thinking about what the future held. The holidays would be here before you know it, would she get a ring? Would they spend Christmas day together? What would their kiss be like at the drop of midnight, ringing in the New Year?

It was as though all of her dreams were coming true. Her daughter was becoming a lovely young lady. Her writing flowed with emotions. She was about to begin her book tour. Now her personal life was becoming complete.

She took his hand and brought it closer to her neck, hugging it tightly. He moved closer, pulling her into him.

"Go back to sleep, baby, it's too early to be awake," he whispered softly into her ear.

It was a bit early, she closed her eyes and fell back to sleep.

♦

The sun was just beginning to rise. Daniel had turned from her and was facing the other direction. She quietly slid out of bed and walked into the bathroom, closing the door behind her.

She was washing her hands when her eyes looked over at her toothbrush. Maybe it was habit, or her devious mind throwing out an idea, either way she picked it up, placed paste on it and brushed her teeth before heading back to bed.

She gradually opened the door, but it made a light creaking noise. She froze. Daniel moved a little in bed, but did not seem to awaken. She shimmied out of the small opening and tip toed back to bed.

She slowly crawled between the covers. Daniel was now lying on his back. She slithered under the covers and found his cock. It was flaccid. She didn't recall ever seeing it that way, but it was still a decent size.

She took his balls in her hand, using her thumb to lift his head to her lips. Her mouth began caressing it, manipulating with her tongue. She felt it become engorged. She began moving it in and out when she felt the covers being tossed to the side.

"Fuck, sexy, what a great way to wake up."

"Imagine this every day."

"That would be heavenly."

"I can't think of a better way to wake up."

"Bring that ass up here so you can enjoy."

She did as she was told, even though she was already enjoying. Knowing she was satisfying him was all she needed.

He began to finger her pussy. She was extremely wet. They both began to moan softly, her moans added to his pleasure. She was completely engrossed in his dick. Try as he might, he couldn't get her to cum.

"Get on all fours."

She pulled away from him and assumed the position, facing the headboard. He knelt between her knees and lined up his tip with her hole. He slid it in slowly until her ass was against his groin.

He ground his hips against hers. Now he had her attention. He pulled back and began working just the head. She loved that tease. Her whimpers increased. He knew she wanted his full shaft, but not yet. He remained constant until she began to scream.

He pushed fully into her. Primal sounds emanated from her throat as he pounded into her cunt. She could hear the splashes as his body smacked against hers while her juices flowed.

He grabbed her hips and pulled them as close as he could. He released his cum deep inside, howling as he did.

He held her in position beyond his orgasm, as she was still riding out hers. Wave after wave of strong emotions was overtaking her body. She buried her head in the pillow and cried out.

As her voice went silent, he gently placed her in the bed and went for a washrag. Tears began running down her cheeks. Her orgasm had brought something to the surface. She wiped her eyes as she heard Daniel coming back into the room, not wanting him to know.

He placed the cloth between her legs and kissed her forehead, "You clean up. I'm going to throw on some clothes and start making breakfast. Take your time."

He grabbed his pajamas and went into the bathroom before going to the kitchen. She began to cry once again as he left.

What is going on? Why am I crying? Everything is perfect, why the waterworks?

She had no good answers, so she just went with it. She let the emotions flow. They only lasted a minute or two. When they were gone, she felt a relief. Of what, she wasn't sure.

She got out of bed, placed the rag in the bathroom and put her negligee on before heading out into the kitchen to help Daniel with breakfast.

She walked into the room and put her arms around Daniel. "A man in the kitchen is the sexiest thing I could imagine."

"Even more than a buff, topless firefighter holding a puppy?"

She pursed her lips and thought about that for a moment. "Hmm, that's a tough one. While I can't resist a puppy, I still need to eat. Now, if he were holding the puppy while flipping some eggs; that might be sexier."

They laughed. She kissed him on the cheek and opened the cabinet to grab glasses. She took them to the fridge and poured out the orange juice. She set them in front of the barstool at the island. Daniel had his coffee, so she grabbed a mug and filled it with her vice.

Daniel was busy with his fried potatoes. Stephanie asked what she could do to help. He told her he was good and suggested she check her messages in case Brianna needed her.

She walked into the bedroom and took the phone from the charger. She did have two messages, but neither were from Brianna, they could wait. She put her phone in her suitcase and headed back to Daniel.

"Everything good at home?"

"I'm guessing it is, she didn't text me. She's growing up so fast, she really doesn't need me anymore."

Daniel turned toward her, "Honey, she will always need you. Her needs will just change. Get ready, it will soon go from you being the grocery store to being the bank; and the withdrawals will be astronomical!"

She smiled, "Oh, I have no doubt. The days of the $10 a week allowance are long gone."

He laughed, "You were generous, my kids got $1."

"I find that hard to believe. Your children are not that much older than Brianna."

He put his hands on his hips, "Gorgeous, I have grandchildren."

"Okay, so maybe they are a little older, but I'm sure you were very generous."

"Oh, I was generous all right. My wife bought them anything they wanted. You wonder why I'm successful, it's because I had to keep ahead of her!"

They chuckled as he began the eggs. A few minutes later, Daniel was plating the breakfast and putting it on the island.

He sat next to her. He lifted his glass as to make a toast. "Here is to another wonderful day with a gorgeous woman."

They clinked glasses and took a sip. They ate their meal with a bit of lighthearted conversation. When they finished, Stephanie took the plates to the sink and began washing them. Daniel grabbed a towel and dried.

"Your mother taught you right. She definitely gave you marketable skills."

"Having raised me, she was afraid no one would want me and she didn't want me to starve. She also did not want me living with her forever."

"I see the benefits to her."

When they finished with the dishes, Daniel refilled the coffee. "Honey, why don't you go get our robes and let's sit on the porch."

She grabbed the robes out of the bathroom. When she returned, he helped her slide into hers. He quickly threw his on, and they headed out the door.

The morning was sunny, but a little brisk. Stephanie wrapped her hands around her mug. She was grateful for the dark robe, it pulled in the heat. The woods were still. They sat quietly, sipping the warm liquid, breathing in the fresh air.

"It's a beautiful day," Stephanie commented.

"Yes it is. How would you feel about a little walk through the woods?"

"Would it be like the last stroll?"

"No, I mean a real walk. I can show you a few spots that are breathtaking. They are great places to go and think."

"Sounds like a nice way to spend the day."

They continued to soak in the sun until their coffees were empty. Daniel took Stephanie's hand and led her into the house. He placed their mugs in the sink and walked back to the bedroom.

Daniel pulled an outfit from a drawer. Stephanie dug through her suitcase to see what would be appropriate for their adventure. Jeans were going to have to work, wandering around the woods was not something she had prepared for.

"Honey, don't waste a pair of jeans on this. Let me give you some sweats," he pulled another set of clothes out of his drawer and gave it to her. "They might be a little big, but they will be comfortable."

"Thank you, baby."

They dressed, but before they left, Stephanie headed into the bathroom. She wanted to at least put on a little eyeliner and mascara, just in case they ran across the neighbors. Daniel shook his head when she returned.

"Trying to look good for the bears?"

"If that's the last name of your neighbors, then yes."

"After yesterday, I'm sure they won't be looking at your face."

"Haha, let's go."

They left the cabin and headed out on their jaunt.

Daniel had been correct. The views were majestic and there were many little knobs where you could sit on a rock and see all around the lake.

While venturing onto a boulder, they looked down to the lake and saw a bear in the water apparently looking for lunch. Stephanie was relieved to know that there was quite a distance between it and her.

They walked about a quarter of the way around the lake before turning back. It was an enjoyable way to spend a few hours. They chatted about many things, including their childhoods. She was very pleased with his choice of the morning activity.

CHAPTER 14

D ANIEL OPENED THE DOOR to the cabin. "Let's get showered before the game."

"What game?"

"The football game."

"Oh."

"Let me guess, that's not the way you spend Sunday afternoons."

"Well, not as a single woman. That's usually my cleaning day."

"There is nothing here for you to clean, so you can sit and watch the game with me."

"You have a point. Just don't be upset if I drift off."

"As long as you don't get upset when I scream at the screen and wake you."

She chuckled, "Deal."

They were now in the bedroom. Daniel went looking for an outfit while Stephanie headed into the bathroom.

She began running the water, allowing it to warm before she stepped in. She undressed and threw Daniel's clothes in his hamper. She checked the water temperature, then entered the shower.

The water felt wonderful rolling down her body. Her eyes were closed, head tilted back under the flow when she heard a rustling. She remained statuesque, knowing it was Daniel.

A moment later, the shower door opened and he slid in. She stepped aside and let him enjoy the water. He rinsed off before turning his attention to her.

He pulled her under the spray, holding her close and kissing her deeply. Now this was how showers went when he was around.

His hands wandered over her body, lingering at the more important places. She began rubbing against him. His hands were on her ass, pulling her close to his erection. She felt his excitement.

He continued to kiss her as he placed a hand between her thighs. It wandered past her lips and into her pussy. His other hand split her crack and a finger pushed against her anus. Her hands were on the sides of his head as she began kissing him even more deeply.

He now had fingers in both holes. The one in her ass stayed still as a second finger joined the first in her pussy. He bent over and began pumping her hole vigorously. She grabbed the sides of the shower, anchoring herself as her passion began. She lifted one leg, allowing him to get deeper. His palm was smacking her clit. The sensation drove her to a deep orgasm.

He continued until she had to pull away. Her legs were shaking. She could barely stand. She was breathless.

Staring into his eyes, she knelt on the shower floor. His cock was in front of her. She took it in her hand and began jerking it back and forth. It was a slow movement, buying her time to regain her composure.

He grew tired of her hand quickly and placed his dick in her mouth. He could give himself a handjob; he didn't need one from her. He grabbed handfuls of hair and pumped his hips.

She wasn't quite ready for him and began to gag. He continued relentlessly. She placed her hands on his hips and tried to slow the pace so she could catch her breath. It worked. She took her hands away when she was ready for his shaft in her throat.

Her hands were behind her back, finger entwined. She had assumed the position. He pulled her in and held her face to his groin.

He loved the feel of his head hitting the back of her throat and sliding down. When she began to gag, he pulled back and moaned. He pulled his shaft out, gave her a moment, then shoved it back to that sweet spot, this time holding it longer.

He was so aroused. He wanted to cum, but held it. He wasn't going to finish in her throat.

He grabbed her arm and stood her up. He told her to lift her leg and he put his arm under it. He lined up his cock and plunged into her. She gasped. He pumped her pussy, telling her to look him in the eyes. He wanted to see her orgasm.

She was just about to hit her climax. He continued telling her to look at him, as she topped the pinnacle and he exploded inside her. They stared at each other and moaned loudly. He had timed it perfectly.

He let her leg go and held her tight, kissing her gently on the top of the head. He didn't let go until he was sure she was stable enough to stand on her own.

He placed her under the water and began washing her hair. He ran his fingers through her long locks, rinsing it thoroughly.

She took the bar of soap and began washing his body. This time he didn't mind when her hand was on his dick. They switched places, he washed his hair and rinsed while she washed her body. He got out of the shower while she rinsed.

He dried off and handed a towel to her as she exited the stall.

Daniel went into the bedroom to dress before heading into the kitchen to get their game day snacks and drinks prepared. Stephanie still needed to finish her makeup. She ran her hands through her hair, shook it up, and decided that would have to do.

She headed to the living room. Daniel was bringing the spread of food and placing it on the coffee table as she sat down.

"Are we having guests?"

"No, why would you ask that?"

"That's a lot of food for just the two of us."

Daniel had prepared a tray of cheese and crackers, brought out bags of chips, pretzels, and corn chips with a salsa. He had placed a few beers and her bottle of wine in a bucket filled with ice that he placed on a towel on the floor.

"I don't expect us to eat everything; I just didn't want to get up during the game."

"That makes sense."

"Shall we wager?"

"I guess we could. What were you thinking?"

"The losing team at halftime has to give the winning team head."

"So I'm guessing you are referring to us when you say team. That would certainly make for an interesting half time show if were the players."

"It might get them to play better."

"Or not…"

Daniel gave a hearty belly laugh and kissed Stephanie on the cheek. "You have such a devious mind."

"That's what keeps you coming back."

He was putting a cracker in his mouth as she spoke. He nearly choked. "Alright, sexy, your team is in the blue, mine are in the red."

"So I don't get to pick?"

"No. That's my team and I would not bet against them."

They sat back and watched the game. At first Stephanie seemed disinterested. She drank her wine and nibbled on some cheese. She hadn't fallen asleep, but she had been very quiet.

They came to the end of the first quarter with Daniel's team up by a touchdown.

"Shall I start opening my pants?"

"It's only the first quarter. A lot can happen before halftime."

"Yes, we can score many more times by then."

"That doesn't sound like you are trying to score here. I think you might be surprised with who gets head at half time."

"Shall we up the ante?"

"What were your thoughts?"

"Losing team gives head and then has to undress and sit naked for the second half so the winning team can do as they wish."

She thought about the possibilities for a moment. "What limits are you putting on this?"

"No blood, no watersports, no extreme pain."

"So there could be minor pain and humiliation?"

"Yes."

"I'm in. Just remember this was your idea."

"Now who is the cocky one?"

"Not cocky, confident."

"Alright, sexy, just remember you will pay for that confidence."

She began paying more attention during the second quarter. While still drinking her wine and nibbling, she began cheering for her team. Daniel was surprised by her knowledge of the game.

"I thought you didn't like football?"

"I don't. This is not how I would choose to spend a Sunday afternoon."

"You seem to understand the game pretty well."

"I do. When I was married, I had to sit and watch it every time the home team played. After all those years I began to understand the game. It got to the point where the last couple of years he would suggest I find something else to do so he could watch the game in peace."

"What did I get myself into?"

"Live and learn, baby, live and learn."

"There's always something new to learn with you."

She gave him a smirk, "You have no idea."

Daniel had no idea what secrets Stephanie kept hidden. She seemed like an open book, but it only went so far. There were many things she kept to herself. It would take years for him to get behind the gates. She had opened a few for him, but there were many more. She would like to let him in, but her fears wouldn't allow it.

They continued to watch as the teams battled between the twenties. Sacks, interceptions and dropped passes plagued both teams. If only her team could get it together and score. Her chances of being the victor at half time were not looking good.

There were 30 seconds left in the first half. Daniel's team was on the 30 with a third and five. The quarterback dropped back for a short pass to the sideline hoping to get the first down and stop the clock. The ball sailed over the line directly toward the intended receiver.

Five feet before the ball could be caught, Stephanie's defense picked it out of the air and began running down the field. Daniel's players pursued the defenseman and brought him down at the two-yard line.

Daniel was very pleased by his team's performance. Ten seconds on the clock, one play and it would be over.

The snap, the quarterback looks to pass, no openings. He does the only thing he can; he jumps up and over, extending the ball as far as possible. He was knocked down, but not before the line judge lifted his arms – Touchdown!

Stephanie jumped off the sofa and began loosening her jeans.

"What are you doing?" Daniel asked with a smirk.

"Getting ready for my oral."

"You aren't winning. The best you can hope for is being tie."

"That just means we both need to perform. I still need my pants off," by this time she was pushing her panties down to the floor.

Her team lined up and kicked the extra point – the score was flat.

Daniel stood and began removing his pants. "Lay down on the rug."

That had already been her plan. She lay there on her back, legs spread and arms up waiting for his hips to be over her face.

Daniel knelt on the floor. She immediately began touching his cock, arousing it more before beginning. He pushed her legs further apart before diving between them. He immediately began to devour her pussy.

His dick was solid as she slid it past her lips. Her head began to bob up and down, working the shaft.

Daniel knew their time was limited. His arms were wrapped around her thighs. He began fingering her as his tongue and teeth worked her clit. He began pumping his hips, forcing the head into her throat.

She was fully aroused. He pulled his manhood from her, began humming while pounding her cunt. Her back arched and she moaned deeply as the orgasm washed over her.

The game was ready to begin again. He straightened up, looked into her eyes, and said, "Are you ready for the second half?"

She was a little woozy, but responded, "I think I need a minute."

He chuckled and stood up. He dressed and sat on the sofa. She was still on the floor catching her breath. A few moments later she popped up, put on her panties, then sat next to him.

"Didn't you forget something?"

"Nope, no reason to put on what I will be taking off soon anyway."

"Always thinking ahead."

"Always."

They continued watching the game.

♦

The second half began with Daniel's team scoring a touchdown, but both teams fizzled after that. They looked like peewee teams. Many of the fans at the game had left by the middle of the fourth quarter. It was a relief when the buzzer sounded the end of the game.

"That was non-climactic," Stephanie commented to Daniel.

"Yes, it was," he put his arms around her. "Aren't you glad halftime wasn't anti-climactic?"

She smiled, "Yes I am."

For the next fifteen minutes they spooned on the couch. It was time to connect. They had physically joined many times this weekend, now it was emotional. The energy between them led her to orgasm. She had not felt this chemistry with anyone before. It was what she had been searching for.

Daniel pulled away, "Are you ready for dinner?"

"Are we talking about food or sex?"

"Food, silly."

"Don't you think we should work up an appetite first?"

"You are a horny little bitch, aren't you?"

"Would you prefer that I wasn't?"

"Certainly not, but our time is limited. I have some steaks I was going to throw on the grill. I was thinking mashed potatoes and peas, how does that sound?"

"Sounds good. What do you need me to do?"

"Just help me out with peeling the potatoes."

They went into the kitchen. She peeled potatoes as he seasoned the steaks and placed them back in the fridge. While the potatoes were boiling, Daniel washed up the dishes and Stephanie dried them.

They talked while waiting to start the steaks. Stephanie began thinking about her upcoming schedule; it would be weeks before she would have the opportunity to repeat this weekend. She wanted to remember every minute.

Daniel mashed the potatoes and put them in the oven to keep warm. He was ready to throw the steaks on the grill. Stephanie went to the sofa and picked up her jeans, putting them on before heading out with Daniel.

The steaks were on the grill when she walked over to him.

"You didn't need to come out here."

"Yes I did."

She got down on her knees and opened his pants. She had told him many times that if he cooked she would suck his cock as he did. It was time to reward the actions she wanted him to repeat.

Her mouth showed her appreciation as he flipped the meat. He nearly burnt the steak, getting so caught up in the feeling of her lips against his groin. He grabbed her head as he mustered up another load, fucking her face until his jizz shot down her throat.

She drank every drop, licking her lips as his dick dislodged.

"Thank you," she said.

"I should be thanking you."

He put the steaks on a plate and took them in the house.

The peas still needed to be opened and placed in the microwave. Stephanie handled that as Daniel prepared their plates. They sat at the island for dinner.

The conversation was light. They discussed a few networking events and meetings they had coming up this week. She would not be seeing him before her book signings. They knew that the next few months would be difficult to see each other. They agreed that it might need to just be a quickie here and there, but they would survive.

They finished their meal and cleaned up the kitchen. It was now time to pack things up and get ready to head home.

She was feeling a bit melancholy. It had been a wonderful weekend, but all good things must come to an end. She needed to focus on the bond that had strengthened, not that she wouldn't be seeing him for some time.

"Positive, Stephanie, think positive," she continued to repeat in her mind.

Her bag was packed; she was ready to head home and get ready for the busy week in front of her. She also needed to catch up with Brianna.

"All ready to go?"

"No."

"No? What do you need?"

"More time with you."

He wrapped his arms around her, "Honey, we have lots of time. I'm not going anywhere."

They had a small peck, then headed out the door. He helped her into the car, put their bags in the trunk, and began their trip home.

CHAPTER 15

T HE RIDE HOME WAS QUIET, just soft music in the background. They held hands the whole way. Daniel kissed her hand as he pulled the car into her driveway. He grabbed her suitcase before opening her door. They kissed good-bye at the car. She walked into her house alone.

"Hello," she yelled after she closed the door. She wasn't surprised that there was no answer. She left her suitcase at the bottom of the stairs and sent Brianna a text.

I just got home, come down and chat.

She went into the kitchen and looked in the pantry for some hot chocolate. The weekend reminded her that it had been a long time since she and Brianna wrapped their hands around those chocolaty mugs.

Brianna responded to her message.

I would but I'm not home. Josie and I went for some fro-yo.

Stephanie:

Okay, be careful driving home.

Brianna:

Ugh, you know I will.

Yes, Stephanie did know that Brianna would be careful. She continued searching the closet. Even if they were not going to have any this evening, they should do it soon. Try as she might, she could not find any hot chocolate mix. She would need to stop on the way home from work tomorrow and get some. She should probably buy a few groceries as well.

She began cleaning up the kitchen, not even thinking about messages and emails. Although Brianna was studious in most areas, cleaning up after herself was not one. She wiped down the counters and placed the dishes in the dish washer.

99

She was nearly finished as her phone sounded. She picked it up to see:

I hope I'm not interrupting your weekend, I don't see your schedule in my email. Can you resend it?

Hmm, she thought she had sent the schedule before she left, maybe not. She went into her email and pulled up the message from Maggie and forwarded it to him.

Just sent it over. You aren't interrupting, I just got home.
Zachary:
That's good. I hope you had a great time.
Stephanie:
It was wonderful. I couldn't have asked for anything better.
Zachary:
So, your time with me was not as good?
Stephanie:
I didn't say that. My time with you was completely different.
Zachary:
Different how?
Stephanie:
You were a business trip and this was a romantic get-a-way.
Zachary:
Did you go out to dinner?
Stephanie:
Yes
Zachary:
Did you have a deep conversation?
Stephanie:
Yes
Zachary:
Did you have passionate sex?
Stephanie giggled as she read the question.
Yeeessss
Zachary:
So I still don't see how it was different than your time with me.

Stephanie knew he was joking. He knew how she felt about Daniel, the two did not compare.

Haha.
Zachary:
At least I can make you laugh. I just looked at your schedule and it looks like I might be able to meet you in two weeks. I will double check my calendar tomorrow and make plans.
Stephanie:
You don't have to go out of your way. There are a couple later in the tour that are trade shows, those might be better.
Zachary:
I saw those and if we haven't booked them, I will be sure to get a booth next to you.
Stephanie:
How will you be sure to be next to me?
Zachary:
Let's just say I know a couple of people.
Stephanie:
I think it's more than a couple. I need to let you go, I just heard my daughter get home. Have a great evening!
Zachary:
You too!

Zachary was such a nice man; she really hoped he would find someone to share in his life. In the short time that she had known him, she knew that he was still mourning, but one day he would make a lady very happy. Just like Daniel made her.

Brianna came into the kitchen and placed her purse on the table.

"Well, hello. I cleaned up the kitchen for you."

"Yes I see that. I took care of the laundry."

"You needed clothes, didn't you?" Stephanie snickered.

"I have school tomorrow."

"And of course you have nothing to wear."

"I don't."

Stephanie rolled her eyes, "You poor baby. Doesn't your mother buy you anything?"

"No. She just spends time with men and ignores me."

Stephanie gave her a stern look. "You are far from ignored.

But since you feel that way, we can spend every night this week together. Monday we can have dinner together, Tuesday we can go to the movies, Wednesday we can go bowling and Thursday we can take in an art show."

Brianna cocked her head and lifted her eyebrows. "I don't think so, when would I do my homework?"

"I bet if I changed it to shopping you would go."

"Well, dah."

Stephanie shook her head. "Homework be damned!! So what did you do this weekend? You didn't even message me."

"There were no emergencies and I knew you were busy. Mandy and I went midnight bowling last night and then she stayed over. We slept in and then went to breakfast with her parents."

"Well that was nice. Did you tell her about the upcoming weeks? Will she be able to spend some time with you?"

"We did talk about that and as long as she doesn't have a boyfriend, we are going to hang out."

"Let's hope she doesn't get one for a while. Is there anyone she is talking about?"

"No, she says she is staying single for a year."

"So there will be someone by the end of the month."

Brianna laughed. "Yeah, something like that. Josie was telling me about a college she went to see and I think I want to check it out."

"Okay, you have my schedule. If it's close to where I will be, just plan to go with me that weekend. If we need to make a special trip, just plan it on a free weekend."

"Okay, I don't think it's close to where you will be. I prefer this just be a college trip weekend, not a "Debra" weekend."

"Fair enough. Did you have anything to eat other than fro-yo?"

"No, I ate a lot at brunch. I had been taking a nap when Josie called to see if I could meet her. She needed to talk about boy problems."

"Oh no, not again. Why doesn't she just get rid of him?"

"Because he threatens to kill himself."

"Has she told her father?"

"No, he would freak out. She figures she only needs to put up with it until they go off to separate colleges."

"What if they are at the same college?"

"She is going to lie to him about where she is going, just in case he tries to go to the same school."

"This is insane that she has to deal with this from a kid. Thank God you didn't date him."

"Oh, I know. He has always been strange. I think the time that he found one of your stories was what really did it. Scared him silly."

Their laughter filled the house. She will never forget when Brianna told her what had happened. Brianna was so serious. She had said that Jake had been at the top of the stairs while she ran down into the basement to look for something. Jake had called down to her – Brianna I'm scared. She couldn't imagine what had scared him. She came running over to the stairway to see pieces of paper in his hands. She asked him where they came from and he said he found them on the printer. She told him they were her mother's put them back. He had read one of her erotic short stories.

"I wonder if he still picks up random pieces of paper and reads them?" Stephanie pondered.

"It would be okay to do that at Josie's. It would probably be scripture or a note from her dad."

"Maybe we should slide a story into her dad's briefcase for Jake to find. He would run for the hills. Maybe he would just think we are all freaks and he would never talk to either of you again."

"It's possible. He's not very bright when it comes to those things."

"Well I hope she gets it worked out. College is almost a year away. That's a long time to waste on someone who acts like that. I still think she should tell her dad and have him talk to Jake's parents."

"It wouldn't matter. They would just think she was exaggerating."

"That's unfortunate."

"I'm going to my room. I have a little bit of homework to do before I go to bed."

"Okay, I guess I'll take my laptop and head up, too."

They both climbed the stairs and went into their rooms. Stephanie unpacked her bag and changed into her pajamas. She washed her face and brushed her teeth before climbing in bed.

She opened her laptop and began answering emails. There were a couple of client files she needed to look at before she closed her eyes. She worked on them about an hour before she just could not keep her eyes open.

She closed the laptop and placed it on the floor next to the bed, then rolled over and tucked herself under the covers.

She had just gotten comfortable, nearly asleep when she heard the ding. She reluctantly looked at her phone. She could not possibly carry on a conversation now.

Good night, gorgeous. It was a wonderful weekend. I will let you know when I have time for a quickie.

This would not be a conversation, she was relieved.

Good night, handsome. It was the best weekend of my life.

She again tucked herself in and fell off to sleep.

Chapter 16

T HE PAST TWELVE DAYS had gone by quickly. Maggie had planned well by having the first tour close to home. They learned many things, the biggest being—what not to forget. When Stephanie returned from that trip, she put together a bag that was specifically for this type of travel. She did not want to get caught with her pants down again.

Things with Daniel had continued as they had in the past— morning messages and sexting throughout the day. They had not had an opportunity to see each other since the cabin. Stephanie wanted to see him before she left tomorrow, but it didn't look like that would happen. She would be very busy in her office today and Brianna asked that she go to a program at school tonight. Her stress level had risen, but she was aware and kept it at bay.

Stephanie was at the office when Daniel made his first contact of the day.

Good morning, gorgeous.

Stephanie:

Good morning, handsome.

Daniel:

Are you ready for your weekend?

Stephanie:

I think I am better prepared than last week. Maggie and I have gone over everything forward and back. I can't imagine I could forget anything.

Daniel:

What kind of trouble will you ladies be getting into?

Stephanie:

We won't be getting into any trouble. The only plans we have outside of the convention would be dinner, unless Zachary has something planned.

Daniel:

I don't recall you telling me that Zach would be there.

Stephanie:

I swore I did, but things have been so hectic, I may have forgotten. It's no big deal.

Daniel:

I seem to have found time in my schedule this evening. It's only about 15 minutes, but I could send you off with a smile!

Stephanie:

Ugh! I have to go with Brianna tonight. What is your timeframe?

Daniel:

The employees go home early on Fridays, so I thought you could swing by on your way home. I'll bend you over my desk and fuck the shit out of you.

Stephanie thought about it for a moment. Her schedule was tight and this could make her late getting home, but she really did need to feel him. She could also use the stress relief.

Okay, your office is not exactly on my way home, but I can make it work. I will shoot for getting out of here by five. I'll message you when I leave to make sure your employees have all gone.

Daniel:

Perfect! I will make sure they are out of here, my balls are heavy.

Stephanie:

Okay, handsome, I will message you later. Have a great day!

Daniel:

That's a plan, sexy! You have a good day too.

Stephanie placed her phone on the desk and thought about what he had said. Funny how they had no plans to see each other until she mentioned that Zachary would be there. Could this mean that he was getting jealous? Did he need to "mark" her before she left?

She also locked in on him saying that his balls were heavy. That could only mean that he had not had a release since he came during their phone sex last week. To her, that meant no other women. They really were becoming a couple. She dove into her client files with a smile on her face and lightness in her heart.

Throughout the morning she was focused on getting the clients up to date and making sure Pam understood all aspects of each client in preparation of her being off two days the following week to go with Brianna to visit a couple of colleges.

Just before she was ready to run out for lunch, she got a message from Brianna.

Is everything set up for next weekend? I just talked to someone in my last class that visited last weekend. He was told that they had a lot of applications already and were filling up fast. I really want to get my application in.

Stephanie:

Relax, I'm sure they told him that because they wanted to create a sense of urgency. We are still very early in the year for them to be getting full. I would think that by him being told that the college is actually behind in applications.

Brainna:

But what if they really were telling the truth?!?! I don't want to be left out of a school I really like.

Stephanie:

If this is the school you are supposed to go to, you will get in. You might not even like it when you get there. I don't see the need to waste all this money on application fees for a bunch of different colleges like some of your friends do. I'm an accountant, remember?

Brianna:

Fine! Just remember I will not forgive you if I don't get in.

Stephanie:

I'll take that chance. Relax and get back to class, I'll be home at six.

Brianna:

We need to leave at six! Why is it going to take so long to get home? You are finished at five.

Stephanie:

I will be home by six at the latest. I will shoot for earlier, but you know how things go. I could get an important phone call as I am ready to leave. Just relax, I know my timeline.

Brianna:

Okay, but don't be late.
Stephanie:
I will not be late.
Great, nothing like adding more to her overloaded plate. She needed to be sure to get out no later than 4:45. His employees had best not be lollygagging around the office, or they were going to be in for a show.

She sent a quick text to Daniel letting him know she would be a little earlier than expected and to be sure everyone was gone. She needed to condense her day, so eating while working would have to do. She went out to grab a sandwich.

The sub shop was only a few blocks away. As she walked, she hoped that she had missed the lunch crowd. She opened the door to see a small line. She stood behind the last person and began checking emails on her phone.

A voice from behind her said hello. She didn't recognize it at first, so she continued responding to emails.

The person tapped her on the shoulder. "Are you ignoring me?"

When she turned, she realized that it was her neighbor of many years ago. She had not seen him in at least five years.

"Oh my God, I'm so sorry. I didn't recognize your voice at first."

"I see you have forgotten all about me."

"No, I would never do that. Today is just one of those days. Too much to do, too little time to do it."

"I know the feeling. How is Brianna?"

"She's beginning to check out colleges. We have our first visit next week."

"Time is flying by so fast. I remember when she was born."

"Tell me about it. How are your girls?" Stephanie placed her order as he spoke.

"They are doing well. Now that they are all grown, I don't get to talk to them very much. Their mother was not very kind where I was concerned either."

"That is so unfortunate. You were a great dad. I remember

you helping Brianna with her bicycle. Divorce is a cruel thing. Why do people need to be so nasty?'

"Because they can't accept responsibility."

Stephanie's sandwich was ready, "You're probably right. Hey, I need to get back to the office, stay in touch."

He hugged her, "I will."

Stephanie left the shop and power walked back to her office. Pam would be leaving in less than three hours—she needed to be sure everything was in order. She looked over the list she had prepared and found two things that still needed to be discussed. They worked on those items before Pam left for the day.

Stephanie cleaned the files from her desk and was ready to head out the door. She shot Daniel a quick message.

I'm finished, heading out the door right now.

She locked up the office and headed to her car. As she started the ignition, Daniel responded.

Coast is clear, I will be in my office stroking my cock.

She wasted no time getting to his office. She parked the car, grabbed her fob and headed inside. He had left the door open; she locked it before heading to his office.

He was facing the door, pants open with his erect penis in his hand, stroking slowly. Her eyes were immediately drawn to his dick like radar.

"Get rid of everything from the waist down, except your shoes."

She closed his office door and began to strip as she walked toward him. She took off her shoes to remove her pants, but placed them back on her feet when she was free of the garments. She took off her jacket and placed it on a chair. She now stood half naked in front of him.

He took his empty hand and slid it between her thighs. She wasn't ready. With limited time, he wasted none of it and immediately placed his fingers in her vagina. She gasped and closed her eyes. He manipulated her hole only a few moments before she was slippery and ready for his entry.

He stood, pushing his chair back as he did. "Bend over the

desk."

She turned and placed her hands on the desk as she leaned forward and stuck out her ass. He placed his head against her pussy and pushed it in.

She gave an appreciative moan and lifted her bum higher. He moved his arms around her, unbuttoning the top couple of buttons. He pulled her breasts over the top of her bra just enough to get to her nipples. He squeezed them hard while slowly stroking.

He grabbed her hair and thrust hard. She screamed, a smirk came across his face. He lifted her right leg onto the desk. He grabbed her hips and began pounding her wide open hole.

Her tits bounced forward and back. She pulled her head down and then threw it back as she moaned loudly. Her orgasms were constant, his balls were wet.

He glanced at the clock on his desk. She only had a few more minutes.

"Are you ready for my cum, baby?"

In a breathy voice, she answered, "Yes I am. I want all you have."

"Okay, sexy, get ready."

He stroked five times before driving his shaft deep inside, exploding. He emitted a noise that was somewhere between a moan and howl. She whimpered and stayed still.

He didn't move until he caught his breath. With his hands on her bum, he watched as his cock slid from her. He went over to the credenza and grabbed a few tissues, using one on himself and giving the others to Stephanie.

She wiped away as much of him as she could, then began dressing.

He closed his pants. "That might have been fast, but it was great!"

"Yes, it certainly was," she kissed him as she walked past to grab her pants.

"Are you ready for the weekend?"

"Yes, I think we are. It's going to be very busy. Monday will be a tough day in the office."

"Just focus on the goal."

"That's what keeps me going." She was dressed and fixing her shirt. She walked over to him and kissed him deeply.

"I knew something was missing. Good luck with your trip. Let me know how things go."

"Thank you. I will keep you posted."

He placed a peck on her forehead and patted her ass as he walked her to the door. She headed to her car with a commanding stride.

She quickly got in, started the car, then drove off, she had twenty minutes to get home. As she drove, she could feel his juices leaking from her. She would need to change before heading out. She drove a little faster, trying to leverage every possible moment.

She opened the garage door, but did not pull the car in. They would be leaving in just a few minutes. She rushed into the house and up the stairs. Brianna heard the garage door.

As they passed in the hall, Brianna asked, "Where are you going? We need to leave."

"I'll just be a minute. I want to change into something more casual. Get your things together and wait for me in the car."

"Just make it quick."

"I will. Relax." Stephanie went into her closet and grabbed a pair of underwear, pants, and a sweater. She went into the bathroom. As she stripped, she threw her clothes in the hamper. She didn't have time to shower, so she grabbed a feminine wipe to clean her pussy. She squeezed the walls of her vagina to remove as much cum as possible. She grabbed a panty liner and dressed.

It was less than five minutes until she was back in the car with Brianna. They headed off to the coffee house performance.

"How long will we be here?"

"It usually lasts an hour and a half."

"Oh, I thought it would be longer. Are we going to get something to eat afterward, or will you be going with your friends?"

"There will be a bunch of us going out, but you're allowed to come."

Stephanie giggled, "Glad you got approval."

They were one of the first to arrive at school. Stephanie took a seat in the "parent" section. She sat quietly as the other parents and students arrived. She was not familiar with their faces, so she took the opportunity to relax. The next few days would be very busy, so this was a great escape.

When the performance began, student after student went to the microphone and belted out familiar songs, each one worthy of being on stage.

Stephanie was impressed by how many talented students belonged to this small school. There were many opportunities for these children to explore and use their talents within the safety of their peers.

Stephanie was very impressed with Brianna and Josie's duet. Too bad Josie's dad hadn't come to watch the performance; at least there would have been one familiar face. No matter, she still enjoyed the show, cheering and clapping after every performance.

After the show, they went to dinner as planned. Stephanie tried to check her phone, but Brianna gave her that look. Stephanie listened to the children and chimed in on occasion. When the conversation waned, the group disbursed and headed home.

Brianna headed to her room and Stephanie to hers. Stephanie still had some packing to do before heading to bed. She would be leaving early, their flight was 8 am.

She finished and went to Brianna's room.

"I'm going to leave early, is there anything you need?"

"No, I have everything in order. I have a big project due Monday, so I will work on that. Mandy will be over after work tomorrow and be here until you get home."

"Sounds good, you can always call your aunt if you need anything right away. I'm not going to be able to answer messages during the show."

"I know. We are fine by ourselves. We will probably have a pizza night, maybe go get some Chinese or tacos."

"Okay, I transferred some money into your account. If you need more, let me know."

"We have money, if we need it."

"Yes, I know you do."

Stephanie went back to her room and got ready for bed. She had everything in order, time to get some sleep.

She plugged in her phone and checked messages. Maggie had reminded her to check in to her flight, a couple of girlfriends had wished her luck, and Daniel messaged her good night.

She sent Maggie a screen shot of her boarding pass, thanked her girlfriends and mixed in a little small talk, then she sent Daniel a text.

Good night, handsome. Thank you for a lovely afternoon delight!

Daniel immediately responded.

You're welcome sexy, can't be sending you off in a state of longing.

Stephanie:

Maybe I need to go away to meet other men more often.

Daniel:

Haven't you been doing that every weekend lately?

Stephanie thought about that a moment. Yes she did see men during her other weekends, yet he did not feel the need to give her this send off. This trip was different—Zachary was going to be there. Could Daniel be feeling threatened?

You're right, I have been. You owe me more send offs.

Daniel:

I will remember that. I'll put it in my schedule.

Stephanie:

That would be fabulous!

Daniel:

LOL, good night, sexy.

Stephanie:

Good night, handsome.

CHAPTER 17

HER ALARM SOUNDED before the break of dawn. She had loaded her luggage in the car last night, giving her a few more minutes of sleep. She hurriedly brushed her teeth, jumped in the shower, and threw on some traveling clothes. She didn't waste much time on makeup, she would do that later.

She opened Brianna's door, just a crack and said goodbye. Brianna moaned back at her. She grabbed a quick drink of water before heading into the garage and jumping in the car. She was picking Maggie up on the way.

As she was pulling out of the driveway, her phone sounded. She was sure it was Maggie making sure she was underway. She glanced to see it was from Zachary.

Good morning! I was thinking about the trip last night and realized that I should have had my plane take you and Maggie. It would have been a quick stop and you would not have had to get up so early.

Stephanie thought about that statement. He was right, it would have been easier. Why didn't one of them think of this sooner?

Good morning! That would have been a good idea. We need to remember it for next time.

Zachary:

I will make a point of discussing it with Maggie while you are busy with your flock.

Stephanie:

LOL, my flock. I don't see myself as a spiritual leader.

Zachary:

You are leading them into their depravity, safely. You create an outlet for them to allow their secret pieces to see the light of day. That is no small feat.

Stephanie:

I just write, it's no big deal.

Zachary:

You are a big deal; ask anyone you speak with this weekend. You do things others only dream about.

Stephanie:

Okay, whatever, I need to get Maggie and coffee. I'll see you in a few hours.

Zachary:

Yes, you will. Safe travels!

Stephanie:

Thank you!

Stephanie pulled into the drive-thru line and ordered their coffees. They would only be mediums today. They needed to finish them before going through TSA. It would kill her to throw away her coffee.

She had their caffeine infusions and would be at Maggie's in two minutes. Her phone began to ring.

"Hello, I'm almost there. I just got coffee."

"Okay, just making sure. I'll be waiting outside."

As Stephanie pulled into the driveway, she saw Maggie stepping off the porch with her carry on and oversized purse. Maggie had the promotional material sent directly to the venue, saving them energy and time. They would be able to just get on the plane without stopping to check bags.

Stephanie parked in the short-term lot and they caught a bus to the terminal. They easily went through security and headed to the gate.

As they walked Maggie commented, "Did you see the smile you got from the guy checking the security screen?"

"What are you talking about?"

"When you stood in the full body scanner, he looked at the screen and then smiled in your direction. I guess he liked what he saw."

"That's bullshit, they can't see anything."

"I don't know about that, he looked pretty happy. I would

know for sure if the machine would not have been in front of him."

They both laughed loudly. Others walking through the concourse turned their heads and looked at them. They paid no mind. They did as they pleased and if others didn't like it, too bad. Maggie and Stephanie were living life to the fullest.

When they got to the gate, Stephanie sat with their bags as Maggie went to get them a real cup of coffee.

Stephanie took out her phone and sent a text to Brianna letting her know they were at the airport and the flight was on time. While she was preoccupied, a man sat next to her and began to speak.

"Good morning, what gets you up so early this morning?"

"My girlfriend and I are travelling for business. She went to grab us coffee."

"Girlfriend? Do you travel together often?"

Should she? The man was very attractive, but it was a bit early in the morning. She took a look at his left hand, there was a ring. She was going for it.

"Yes, girlfriend. We travel almost every week. It's great to have sex in different cities. Keeps things alive, you know?"

"I can see how that would be exciting," he fidgeted in his seat.

"Especially if someone else joins us."

Maggie walked over to Stephanie, not hearing the conversation. "Can we sit over here, alone, so we can talk about the plan for today?"

Stephanie stood, "Sure we can." She turned back toward the man, "Can I get your card? Maybe we could have a drink… or something."

The man fumbled to find a card. "Certainly, give me a call anytime."

"Thank you, I will."

The women walked about ten feet away and sat down. Maggie was the first to speak.

"What was that about? Was he hitting on you?"

"I think he would have, but I saw his ring first. I told him that you were my girlfriend and we traveled to have sex in different cities with other people."

Maggie tried not to burst out laughing. She bumped her coffee cup against Stephanie's.

"Girl, you are good. Even this early in the morning."

"He deserved it. I bet he has a wife and four kids at home."

"Maybe she's a bitch."

"Maybe. Not my circus, not my monkey."

"So why did you get his number?"

"I wanted to give him a thrill. Who knows, maybe I will give him a call one day, he was cute."

"Oh my god, you are nuts. Now let's talk business."

Maggie and Stephanie went through all the aspects of the day while sipping their coffees. They were able to finish and sit for a few minutes before the plane began to board.

The flight was quick and uneventful. They had two and a half hours before the show began. They grabbed a cab and headed to the hotel. Stephanie checked into their room and Maggie headed to the ballroom to set up for the convention.

Half an hour before the doors opened, Debra took the elevator to the main floor and joined Maggie. They went over a few last-minute ideas, then Maggie went to the room and changed for the show.

Zachary's company had managed to get the space next to her, but he was not yet there. She thought it very odd that he would be late. Debra paced back and forth waiting for the doors to open. She was looking at the floor and playing the day in her mind.

Suddenly, there was a pair of men's shoes in front of her. She looked up to see Zachary standing in front of her with a bouquet of flowers.

"These are for you, dear."

"Thank you. They are gorgeous," she took them from him and kissed him on the cheek.

"I have a vase for you in one of these boxes," he begins digging through the boxes under his table. "Ah, here it is."

"So you had this planned?"

"Of course I did. The only thing I did not plan is that it would take so long to find a florist with just the right arrangement."

"You did not have to do that."

"I know I didn't have to; I very much wanted to."

"You are a wonderful man." She hugged him and put the flowers on the corner of her table.

The doors had opened; it was time to get to work. They spent the remainder of the day talking to fans, taking an occasional break to grab a bite or drink. Before they knew it, the doors were closing.

"What are your plans for this evening?" Zachary asked.

Stephanie looked at Maggie before responding, "I don't think we have any plans other than getting dinner and recapping the day."

"Would you be willing to go on an adventure?"

Stephanie giggled nervously, "Should I be afraid? What are you thinking?"

"Relax, it's nothing bad. I know of an upscale dungeon nearby. I think you would enjoy meeting the Mistress who owns it. Would you like to go?"

Stephanie looked over at Maggie.

"Don't look at me! I'm not into this shit. You're a big girl— you can go on your own. You don't need my permission."

She looked back to Zachary, "Yes, I will go. But you have to take us to dinner first."

"I would take the two of you to dinner either way. Shall we see if we can get a table upstairs or try somewhere else?"

The girls agreed that eating at the hotel would be fine. They were starved. The options for something that would not make them feel lethargic, left them eating carrots and celery all day.

Ninety minutes later, they left Maggie and headed to the valet to get Zachary's rental.

As they drove from the hotel, Stephanie asked, "How long have you had this planned?"

"What do you mean?"

"You rented a car. You must have been planning to take me here, yet you never mentioned it…"

"I had forgotten about the playground, honestly. I received an email the other day from the Mistress. She had seen that the company would be at the show, so she invited me to come over if I was in town."

"Hmm, how well do you know said Mistress?"

"Don't get any ideas. I met her at this exact show years ago. Needless to say, she is a good customer. She wanted me to come and see what she had built, so I went. I was impressed and stopped back a few times since then."

She sat back in her seat, "Whatever you say. I will sit back and watch your interaction. That will tell me all I need to know."

He laughed, "Just because you write seedy stories of lust, doesn't mean it's a representation of life."

She looked over at him, "Oh really. I seem to remember a trip I took a while back that was pretty seedy and full of sex. I believe that was real life, although I guess I could have dreamt it."

"You're right, sexy, it was not a dream."

They sat quietly the rest of the way to the dungeon.

They drove out of town and into a rural area. Zachary turned in a driveway next to an old Victorian home. There was a man wearing a silver chocker collar standing next to the house. He walked toward the car, Zachary lowered his window.

"Ah, Mr. Toyman, have not seen you here in some time. My Lady will be happy to see you again. You may park next to her car."

The man pointed to an open space nearest the door. Zachary parked the car.

"Mr. Toyman? That's the name you use here?" Debra said with criticism.

"No, that is not the name I chose. The Mistress knows who I am. For others, it's just easier to relate me to my products."

Zachary popped the trunk, got out of the car, and opened Debra's door. He took her hand and helped her out. As they walked behind the car, he opened the trunk and took out a large gift bag. Debra continued to wonder just how far things had gone with the Mistress.

The man with the collar opened the door and allowed them to enter as they walked up the stairs to the house. They entered into a small cloak room, then opened a door which took them into the greeting area.

The Mistress was sitting on a tall stool next to the welcome desk. When she saw Zachary, She smiled, stood, and took a few steps toward Him to give Him a hug.

Mistress was a gorgeous, 5'9," mid-thirty-year-old, brunette. She was wearing clear stilettos that increased her height to a commanding 6'3" which made her tower over most of the men. She was wearing a short plastic skirt and an extremely tight corset, her full, large breasts bursting over the top.

"Hello handsome, is that bag for me?" Mistress' voice was very sultry, as were her expressions.

"I brought You a few proto types. I know You will put them to good use and give me a full report."

She giggled deviously, "Oh, You know I will. If My boy behaves tonight, he might be in for a treat."

"I am sure they will perform to your standards."

"Now tell Me, Who is this lovely specimen You have brought with You?" Mistress was looking Debra up and down like a hungry lioness.

"How rude of Me to not introduce Her sooner, this is Debra Darling…"

Before Zachary could complete his introduction, Mistress cut in, "Ah, yes, the writer. I knew Her face looked familiar. Welcome to My playground."

The women shook hands.

"Thank you, Mistress. I was very intrigued when the toy man suggested a visit." Debra smirked and looked toward Zachary as she said "toy man."

"I'm glad he was able to bring you. I want you to feel at home. My playground is Yours. Watch, play, the only thing I ask is that You are respectful to O/others."

"Absolutely, I think I will just observe. I can always use some new material."

The laughed, Zachary took Debra over to the bar area and got Her a drink. He then began to tour her around the house. There was a stage with a stripper pole on the first floor. There was a spanking bench set up, ready for some sort of exhibition.

They walked up a flight of stairs. She glanced into a dressing room as they turned the corner to the bedrooms. There were no doors, just curtains. The rule was if the curtain was closed, it was private play. When the curtain was open—the play could be watched, possibly joined.

The curtain was closed on the first room. They walked past and on to the next room. That curtain was open, and people were playing. Zachary and Debra stopped to view the action.

In the room was a bed with a cage underneath. There was a man in the cage looking at a full-length mirror, allowing him to see what was happening on the bed. There was a Mistress lying on Her back, naked from the waist down. Her legs were in the air, spread wide with another man's face in Her pussy.

As the man watched his Mistress being pleasured by the other man, She told the caged sub how much better the young man was at giving Her head. She completely humiliated Her caged sub, while She enjoyed the fresh lad. Her moans were exaggerated, intensifying the degradation.

"Look at how hard his cock is getting. Don't you wish you had a cock like his?"

"Yes, Mistress."

"Stroke his cock as he satisfies Me."

The submissive in the cage reached his hand out and began stroking the hard cock in front of him.

"Is My boy doing a good job?" She asked the one between Her thighs.

he lifted his head to respond, "The touch is too light."

The Mistress became angry, "How dare you embarrass Me! I taught you better. Do it the right way!"

The sub in the cage grasped the shaft more firmly and

stroked with a rhythm matching the soft music piped through the house. A few moments later the lad began to moan, adding to the enjoyment of the Mistress.

"That's a good boy. Satisfy that dick and you will get your treat."

Both subs continued to satisfy their Recipient. There was a time limit on the room's use and it was running out.

"I must cum before you are allowed to orgasm. Stick your fingers in My cunt!'

The sub pulled his head back and watched his fingers swiftly go in and out of her hole. Her moaning began to escalate; he knew that She would be close. She needed to cum so he could release his balls, he pounded harder. Moments later she screamed announcing Her climax.

She caught Her breath and sat up. "Would you like to cum?"

"Yes, Mistress," the sub softly replied.

"Did you say something?"

He spoke louder this time, "Yes, Mistress."

"How do you ask for permission?"

"Please Mistress, Your boy wants to cum."

"You there in the doorway," the Mistress glanced their way. "Do you think My boy should be allowed to cum?"

Debra put Her hand on Her hip, "Hmmm, I'm not sure he deserves it yet. I don't see him sweating."

"You heard Her. Take his cock in your mouth," she demanded of the caged sub.

With his dick in the submissive's mouth, the young man began to shake; his face became strained as he held back this juice.

"I think he looks ready now, do You agree?"

Debra cocked Her head and walked closer to him. "I'm sure he could wait, but I'm feeling generous. He is ready."

The caged sub released the manhood and the lad began to stroke.

"I will allow you to release your cum onto My sub's face. Make sure to paste his eyes close."

Two strokes later, the young sub began spraying his jizz into the cage and onto the older sub. The Mistress got out of the bed and unlocked the cage.

"Come let Me see you."

The sub crawled out and stood in front of Her, his face cover with cum.

"Lovely, rub it in, hopefully it will get rid of your wrinkles." The mistress turned to walk out the door as she said under Her breath, "One can only wish."

Debra and Zachary had seen the show, it was time to move on. They followed the hall to the next room. The space was available. Debra walked across the room. She stopped in front of the St. Andrew's cross. She extended Her hand to touch it.

Standing there, the memories of Zachary's boardroom flowed into her mind. She closed her eyes and ran the loop through her head. her breathing hastened and slowed as the visions entered her consciousness.

Zachary watched, allowing her to feel the rush of emotions. After a few minutes, he walked up to her, placing His arm around her waist and whispering in her ear.

"You're back in LA, aren't you?"

her eyes remained closed, "Yes."

He pulled her close, "I can take you back there, just say the word."

The reel was coming to an end. she turned to face him, placing her arms around his neck and kissing him on the cheek. T/they held each other. debra pulled back and took Zachary's hand, walking out of the room.

As They walked toward the stairs, They saw that the curtain that had been closed was now open and seemed to be the hot spot. There were three men hovering at the entry, straining to see what was going on.

Debra walked over, "Excuse Me."

The men stood to the side. Debra went into the room where four men were lined against the wall. She turned Her head to see what had their interest.

A Dominant was placing cuffs on a woman and strapping her into a sex swing. It was His wife's fantasy to be fucked by many men, tonight she would take all comers.

Now that she was unable to move, He took a dildo out of His bag, lubed it and placed it in her cunt. He kept it wedged in with His thigh as He pulled out a second, slightly smaller prosthetic. This one was lubed a little more than the first before being placed in her ass. He took one in each hand and began working them in and out of their holes.

The men watching were both in awe and salivating at their chance to plunge their trouser monster in any one of her holes.

The Dom had loosened her holes and was ready to allow the men their chance to get their rocks off.

"My rules are that you must wear a condom; you are allowed to cum in her mouth; you can touch her tits. I suggest you use her hard, that's why she is here – to be your sex toy. She is very experienced, let's hope you are, she needs to be reduced to a puddle."

The first man stepped up, whipped his dick out of his pants, wrapped it and plunged it in her pussy. He was a stallion. Not only was he hung, he lasted. After obliterating her cunt, he slid into her brown hole and owned it.

Two of the men in the door turned and walked away, possibly knowing they could not perform as well.

The stud was still hammering it when the Mistress of the house walked in the room, Her submissive was on a leash, crawling on all fours while wearing a dildo ballgag. Mistress walked over to the man and put Her hand on his shoulder. No words were exchanged, he stepped away, putting his dick back in his pants.

Mistress put Her hand under the sub's chin and lifted his eyes to Hers. "I want you to fuck her hard. Make Me proud."

She stood back as he crawled over and began acting on Her command. With his dildo in the pussy hole, he began jerking his head back and forth.

The Dominant stood near His submissive's head and took

his cock out. He began beating it against her face while smacking her tits. He stuck his lizard in her mouth, pushing out her cheek and hitting it. He began pushing His cock deep in her throat, holding it there until she gagged before pulling it out and doing it again. He reached over and grabbed her breast, squeezing hard.

The woman was overloaded, she was trying to writhe, but had very little movement. Mistress' sub continued jamming his dildo in her hole until they forced her release.

The Dom had shoved his cock deep just as Mistress' collared sub pushed forward, hard. The strapped woman began squirting like a fire hose, soaking the male sub's face and chest.

The Dom pulled his cock out, "Such a good girl... you deserve a special treat... you are making Me so proud."

Mistress gave her sub a paper towel to wipe off, then led him back downstairs.

Debra was quite impressed, maybe even a little jealous, but She too had seen enough and was ready to move on to the next area. She turned toward Zachary and motioned Her head toward the door. They left the room and headed down the stairs.

There was now a male sub tied to the spanking bench. From what they could gather, today was his 70th birthday and he enjoyed spankings. The Mistresses were going to give him 70 spanks as he counted them.

Each Domme picked their paddle of choice. Debra was asked to join in, She chose a paddle with a heart cut into the face. The Mistresses stepped up one by one with Their paddle and swatted his ass five to ten times before stepping back for the next Mistress.

When it was Debra's turn, She placed the paddle on his ass, rubbed it and then pulled her arm all the way back. She made it look as though She was going to swing, but held back. The sub screamed, though he had not been hit. They began making fun of him. Since he was no longer paying attention, Debra did take a good hard swing at his bum and made him feel the pain of misbehaving. The Mistresses continued until his cheeks were red and hot.

When they finished, Debra walked back to Zachary. She was smiling, her face was glowing.

"I think you enjoyed that," Zachary said as He put His arm around Her.

"It was fun, his bottom is so full, lots of options," Debra leaned close to whisper in his ear. "That one Mistress was a bit over the top. She seemed a bit frustrated."

"Agreed. This is an outlet to work on Y/your frustrations, but Y/you need to make sure Y/you can clearly draw the line between play and abuse."

"I guess it depends on the sub as well. For Me, that would be abuse."

"Yes, that's true. I wouldn't use anything but My hand on your bum. I love the feeling of smacking it and then grabbing a handful."

Debra smiled at Him, but did not comment.

"Let Me take you into the basement—that truly looks like a dungeon."

Zachary led Debra through a living room and down some rickety stairs.

"Watch your head, the ceiling is low."

Debra ducked as She took the last stair. The basement had been set up with chains hanging from the ceiling and bolted to the floor. Behind a curtain there was a medical room with a gynecology exam table as the centerpiece.

A wall had been erected to block off an area as an after-care room. There was a bed, without a cage, a lounge chair, and low lighting. There was a female wrapped in a blanket on the chaise.

In another open area, there was a spanking bench, a different design than the one upstairs. A Dominant in a kilt was tying a young woman's wrists and ankles to it. She was wearing only panties.

The Dominant went to His bag of tricks and pulled out a sheathed knife. He stood near the sub and dramatically slid the blade from its covering. He ran the blade flatly down the sub's back. She quivered.

When He got to her underwear, He slid the blade between her skin and the fabric, then pushed the blade, slicing the material. He repeated the act to the other side.

her panties were in His hand as He walked toward her head. He bunched them and shoved them in her mouth.

The Dom grabbed two floggers and began a methodical dance of the fringes on her back. The crowd was growing. Debra moved in front of Zachary to make more room.

There was a pause in action as the Dom plugged in a Hitachi. He motioned to Debra that He wanted Her to join Him. Debra took the vibrator and placed it on the woman's clit.

As Debra monitored the tool, the Dom began using just one flogger, but this time in a rougher play. He ran the fringe through His closed hand before whipping it onto her back. The sub whimpered and moaned.

Debra was slightly bent over the sub's bottom. Thoughts of placing Her fingers deep inside that pussy crossed Her mind, but She had not been granted permission, so She refrained.

The Dominant stepped in front of the submissive and took out her panties. Debra was expecting the Dom to lift His kilt and replace them with His cock, but She was wrong.

"Are you enjoying what the Mistress is doing to you?"

"Yes, Sir."

"Why haven't you thanked Her?"

"Thank you, Mistress."

"Would you like to be allowed to cum?"

"Yes, Master."

"We will continue, and you may orgasm freely."

The Dom and Debra continued with a bit more intensity. Debra smacked and grabbed the submissive's bulbous ass. After a few moments, the sub began shaking and squirting profusely. Debra continued to hold the vibrator on her clit. The Dominant was raking His nails across the sub's back.

When He stopped, Debra took His lead and turned off the Hitachi. The submissive continued to writhe and squirt with no further contact with others.

"I can't stop, this has never happened before."

"Just ride it out, you needed this, baby girl," the Dominant whispered in her ear.

Debra placed the vibrator on the table and the crowd began to clap before disbursing. Debra and Zachary remained with the couple. He was untying the female.

The woman on the chaise walked out of the aftercare room with a blanket for the sub. The five of them had a short conversation where Debra learned that the Dominant was married to the woman in the chaise. The couple often came to the playground to enjoy the thirty something, single mother of two. Normally, the wife would be in Debra's position, but tonight she had needed to be released as well.

The wife was a masochist who used pain to relax after strenuous periods in her life. Her job and ex-husband had been difficult recently and her stress level had been through the roof. T/they were glad that Debra had helped T/them with T/their scene, having another man involved was not what T/they wanted.

Debra expressed Her thoughts on wanting to finger the sub. The woman told Her that it would have been okay and She should do it next time. Debra told her that She certainly would, given the chance. Debra and Zachary said goodbye and headed upstairs.

They got to the top of the stairs and turned the corner where the Mistress was again sitting on Her stool.

"Seems that you were a hit."

"I enjoyed the evening, so many different things going on."

"Yes, tonight is very active, must be full moon. We have these open parties every Friday and Saturday night, feel free to join us anytime you are in the area."

"I will certainly keep that in mind."

They all hugged and wished each other well. Zachary and Debra went back to his car and headed to the hotel.

They talked about what she had seen and how she could

make use of her experience. The conversation was like that of good friends, not one of lovers. She was very comfortable with Zachary, but her weekend with Daniel was still vivid in her mind.

The valet parked the car as the couple headed into the hotel. They got into the elevator. Zachary pressed the button for Debra's floor. She was amazed to think that he would be staying on the same floor and not in the penthouse.

The surprises kept coming as they walked toward her room. Did he really get a room that close to her? Is he across the hall? Certainly, he could not possibly want Maggie to hear them.

They stopped in front of her room.

"You need to get some sleep. Between the convention and the dungeon, I think you have had enough excitement for one day." He placed his hands on her shoulders and kissed her on the forehead.

She was stunned. The only words that came to her were, "Good night, I'll see you in the morning."

Zachary waited for her to get into the room before turning and heading to the elevator, this time pressing the button for the penthouse.

In her room, she thought about what had just happened. It made no sense to her. The only conclusion she could draw was that things would just be business from here out. He could have also been concerned if the staff on this trip found out they had been intimate.

She quietly undressed and readied herself for bed. Maggie was already asleep. Stephanie was not in the mood to talk. Before she rested her head on her pillow, Stephanie plugged her phone into the charger and checked messages. There were none.

She quickly typed one to Zachary.

I had a lovely time tonight, thank you!

Zachary:

You're welcome. Good night

Stephanie:

Good night!

It was very late—she did not want to take a chance of waking anyone, so she decided to wait until the morning to contact Brianna and Daniel.

CHAPTER 18

T HEIR ALARMS WENT OFF in unison. They were not taking the chance of oversleeping. Both women were very groggy, but this was another big day. As they lay in bed debating snooze or getting up, Maggie decided to speak.

"How about you get a shower and I will head downstairs for coffee. It's going to take you longer to get ready."

"I guess that's as good a plan as any."

Both women stretched and threw off their covers. Stephanie headed into the bathroom, as Maggie threw on some sweats and headed to the lobby. Maggie was a take it or leave it gal. She did not feel the need to get all dolled up just to grab coffee.

The water heated quickly and Stephanie, now undressed, entered the shower. The warm water felt great on her face. She stood there motionless for a few minutes reliving the evening before in her mind. She jolted out of the trance as she remembered Maggie would be back shortly. Stephanie was just turning off the shower when Maggie came through the door.

She dried off and placed on a robe before walking out of the bathroom. Maggie was sitting on the sofa with her laptop going through social media.

"There is a buzz about yesterday. The Snapchat filter was a great idea. Definitely worth the money."

"That's good, we need the exposure. We have it for the whole weekend, correct?"

"Yes, we do. I think it was only another $20 for the second day. I thought it was a good way to spend your money."

They chuckled. Stephanie grabbed her phone and began checking emails and messaging Brianna.

Good morning! Is everything going okay?

Brianna:

Yes, everything is fine. Do you know how early it is?

Stephanie:

Yes, I'm surprised you responded. I wasn't planning to hear from you until I was at the show.

Brianna:

I was just trying to fall asleep.

Stephanie:

Fall asleep? Why didn't you do that last night?

Brianna:

We went midnight bowling and then had breakfast. We've been talking since then.

Stephanie:

Alright, get some sleep, I'll be home late tonight.

Brianna:

Okay

She knew the girls would be fine. Now she needed to message the other important person in her life.

Good morning, handsome!

Daniel:

Good morning, gorgeous! You are up bright and early. Didn't Zach wear you out last night?

Stephanie:

No, he did not.

Daniel:

What?!? Is he ill? How could he not want to ravage that body of yours?

Stephanie:

He took me to a dungeon, so I could get some new ideas. It was a very interesting evening.

Daniel:

You will have to tell me all about it, right now I have to finish getting ready for church.

Stephanie:

You know I will! Be sure to ask for a lot of forgiveness!

Daniel:

Is that for you or me? I'm a professional, I don't write erotic novels. Lol

Stephanie:
Haha. You need it just as much as I do.
Daniel:
Alright sexy, I have to go. Make money!
Stephanie:
I am.

It was time to get Debra ready for her awaiting fans. The routine was becoming second nature and going much faster than it had in the beginning. Maggie was ready and waiting when she finished.

"I like that dress," Maggie said. "We should find some time to shop for a few more outfits; we don't want you wearing the same thing every weekend. We can stick with the dark colors. I'm just not sold on the same outfit all the time. You're not Wonder Woman."

"Some days I feel like I am."

"Yes, but that's not what we are going for. Not sure an erotic superhero would work."

They laughed as they walked down the hall. Debra carried a small purse with her phone, mints, and lipstick. Maggie was pulling a bag with all their business necessities.

They entered the elevator. A man and two women were already onboard. The elevator was small. Debra stood close to the man, brushing against him as she turned. She purposely stood closer to him than necessary. She could hear his breathing.

The elevator landed hard on the first floor, causing Debra to lose her balance and fall backward toward the man, pinning him against the back wall. She quickly pushed her hand against him and was able to stand.

"I'm so sorry about that."

The man smirked, "No worries, it wasn't your fault."

They all exited and went in separate directions. Debra looked over her shoulder to see where the man was going and if he was with either of the women.

"What are you looking at?"

"I was checking to see where that man was going."

"Why would you need to know that?"

"I'm just curious. He had a nice package."

"You would know that how?"

"I accidentally placed my hand on it when I was pushing away from him."

Maggie shook her head, "Only you, only you."

"It wasn't my fault the elevator had such an abrupt landing. These shoes are not the most sturdy. I just grabbed the closest thing to me, which happened to be his cock."

"He had arms, possibly his hand, the railing on the wall, there were many other things to choose."

"Yes, but he would not have enjoyed it as much."

"Apparently you would not have either."

"Very true."

They walked into the convention center and to their booth. Zachary's team was already in place, but he was missing. Everyone said their good mornings as the ladies began setting their display.

Debra thought it was odd that Zachary would not be in place for the opening, but soon got caught up with other things and the thought slipped her mind as the steady stream of participants began wandering by.

There was a lull about an hour after opening. Debra looked over for Zachary, but he still had not arrived. She stepped over to his booth.

"Is Mr. Thomas going to be late today?"

"No, he flew home early this morning."

"Oh my, was there an emergency?"

"No, he felt we had things under control and didn't feel it necessary to be here."

Debra tried hard to hide her shock. "Well that is quite the compliment for you, but that is no surprise to me. The two of you were kicking ass yesterday. I expect that this is a profitable event."

"It is. We haven't done it in a couple of years and I think that helped."

"Absence makes the heart grow fonder. I guess that also goes for the vagina and the cock."

They chuckled, "I think even more so."

Debra thought for a moment, "I would have to agree."

She walked back to her booth. She sat and took out her phone to message Zachary.

Good morning! I was expecting to see you this morning. Is anything wrong?

It was only a moment before she got her answer.

Good morning! There is nothing wrong. I thought it would be best if I leave before I did something that might interfere with your relationship.

What could possibly interfere with her relationship? Yes, she and Daniel had gotten closer, but he had not told her that there needed to be monogamy.

I don't think I am following.

Zachary:

You and Daniel have taken your relationship to another level. I can see it on your face and in your messages. You have committed to him and I'm not going to damage that for you. We still have our working relationship and our friendship, that will not change. I will always be here for you.

She had mixed feelings on what he said. She was completely committed to Daniel, but there were feelings for Zachary as well. If she would have been alone, she might have cried.

You are such a sweet man. I can't believe no one has snagged you.

Zachary:

Don't worry, many have tried, it's just not for me. Enjoy the rest of the day and have a safe trip home. Send me a message when you get home.

He really was such a good man.

I will!

Debra decided to take a break and grab coffee for everyone. As she walked, she thought about what he had said to her. She also thought about her relationship with Daniel. Would she be able to commit to only him? Would that be what he wanted? She was unsure of her answers.

She walked back to Maggie, coffees in hand, as another

steady flow of smiling faces began filing through. It was time to get back to work, no more thinking… for now.

CHAPTER 19

S HE WAS COMPLETELY EXHAUSTED as she fell into the chair awaiting her flight. The past two days had been mentally draining. Sensory overload had wiped her out. She needed a break, thank goodness next weekend was just a college visit. When she began this tour series, she thought she was up to the challenge, but she had forgotten what it was like to burn the candle at both ends. Between her accounting practice and the tour, she had not had a day off in weeks. She was relishing the upcoming time with Brianna.

"You look completely wiped," Maggie said from the chair next to her.

"I am. I can't wait for some time off. How much more of this do you have planned?"

"Two weekends, I didn't want to push too much through the holidays. I think we should plan online advertising instead, maybe showing up at a few events or broadcasts. We can evaluate at the beginning of the year and schedule accordingly."

"That sounds great. I need to regroup."

"Schedule yourself a spa day. Getting pampered will do you wonders."

"That does sound fabulous right now. Maybe the first weekend of my break, unless I spend it at the cabin."

"Oh yes, time with "the man," how could I forget."

"Stop it. I know he isn't your favorite, but he treats me like a princess."

"I'll keep my opinions to myself, but princess is not how I feel he treats you. Now, Zachary, he treats you like a queen."

Maggie could see that her comment made Stephanie's mind think for a hot minute, but it soon passed. Stephanie looked at her phone, then pursed her lips.

"Daniel has been very quiet this weekend. I guess he didn't want to be a distraction."

"Or maybe he was distracted," Maggie said under her breath.

"I heard you," Stephanie said as she cocked her head and gave Maggie a look of disagreement.

"I'm sorry, but if he felt like you do, he would have stopped this stupid open relationship bullshit and committed to you and only you. Why does he have such a hard time keeping his dick in his pants?"

Maggie was always one to say what she thought, even if it wasn't at the appropriate time, or place. Stephanie tried not to get uncomfortable.

"I know he has not committed, but I don't think he is seeing anyone else. When does he have the time? He is constantly working and has the other commitments in his life. Hell, he barely has time to see me."

"That's what he tells you. How long can it possibly take to dip his cock? How many times have you just stopped by the office and knocked off a quick one? Do you really think he wouldn't do that with anyone else?"

"Look, I can't stop that from happening. I knew what the rules were going into this."

"Yes, but you weren't in love with him then."

Stephanie drew in a deep breath. "You're right. I didn't think I would fall in love with him. I thought I could handle it. I might have been a bit selfish with the fact that I could have other men. I'm not exactly sure what I was thinking, but the fact remains, I knew the rules."

"Rules can change."

"Yes they can, but I didn't make them to begin with, I just play by them."

At this point Maggie was ready to pull her hair out and bitch slap Stephanie. "You are so frustrating! How is it that you can be such a strong and demanding businesswoman, but when it comes to men, you are reduced to a pile a mush? It just doesn't make sense to me. You deserve better than this. There are plenty of men out there that would give you the respect you deserve. Zachary is just waiting for the opportunity."

"You are full of shit. Zachary will never commit to another woman; he was devastated when his wife passed away. He won't open himself up to that pain again."

"I swear to God you are so oblivious. Do you really think this guy would do what he does for you if he didn't want to be with you?"

"Yes I do. He told me that he was not going to get involved."

"And you believed him? Even after he took you to his home and introduced you to his family?"

"He was entertaining at his home, it was a business party. His family is part of the business."

"Oh my God! I just can't talk to you any longer. I'm going to get a drink. I'll be back before we board."

Maggie abruptly grabbed her purse and headed into the concourse. Stephanie slid down in her seat and placed her feet up on her carry-on. She began thinking about what Maggie had said. She did have valid points, from the outside. Stephanie rationalized that Maggie just didn't know Daniel as well as she did. Stephanie had tunnel vision when it came to Daniel. She had thought about Daniel being with other women, but really didn't see that it was possible. She messaged with him almost constantly. She knew his schedule, Maggie did not. But there was this little voice in the back of her mind that was feeding on Maggie's words. Her insecurities loved hearing the doubts.

The only way to squash them was a text to Daniel:

Hey, handsome! You've been quiet, what are you up to?

While she waited his response, she checked her social media accounts. A few likes, a couple of tweets later, his response popped up on her phone.

Hello there, gorgeous! I was just throwing in laundry and watching football. No rest for the weary.

She switched to messages and answered.

Such a busy man, sounds like you need a little CIP action.

Daniel:

CIP? I'm sorry baby but that escapes me. Something new you learned this weekend?

Stephanie:

Cock In Pussy, handsome. No, it was something that just came across my mind.

Daniel:

Ahh, makes perfect sense. I will remember for next time. Yes I could use some CIP.

Stephanie:

I'd love to be giving it to you now, but I'm waiting to board the plane. Do you have any free time this week?

Daniel:

When I get in the office tomorrow I will check my calendar and we will work something out. We can't let it go too long. Didn't Zach give you enough?

Stephanie:

We did not do anything. He left early this morning to go back to LA. He didn't want to get between us.

Daniel:

Between us?

Stephanie:

Yes, he felt that we had gone to another level and he didn't want to ruin anything. I need to hook him up with someone; he's such a good man.

Daniel:

Well that was nice of him, but you are allowed to enjoy other men. I like hearing the stories.

Stephanie:

I am very satisfied by you. They are calling for boarding. I will let you know when I am home.

Daniel:

Have a safe flight, gorgeous!

Stephanie:

Thank you, handsome!

Stephanie grabbed her bags. She looked around for Maggie. She caught a glimpse of the fiery red hair moving swiftly toward her. She did say she would be back in time to board, Stephanie had not realized that she meant – just in time to board.

Maggie grabbed her carry-on and followed Stephanie to the gate. The ladies sat in their respective seats before Maggie spoke.

"I'm sorry for getting a little gruff earlier. I just don't think he is the right one for you, but I know it's your choice. I'm not going to talk about it on the way home."

"Thank you. I know you are just looking out for me and I appreciate that. As I said, I know what the rules are. I love the feelings I have, if they are wrong and I get hurt, I'll get over it. I just can't believe my heart could be that wrong about this."

"If he hurts you, he will have to deal with me."

"Thanks again. I know you are always there. Now let's hope they turn down the lights and we can get a little shut eye on the way home."

The ladies buckled up and snuggled into their seats as the steward went over the safety rules.

♦

She walked into the boardroom wearing nothing but a fluffy collar and cuffs around her wrists and ankles. A woman dressed in a serving outfit accompanied her. There were five men sitting at a table; one at the head and two flanked each side.

The woman walked her to the table, instructed her to climb onto it, then rolled her onto her back in front of Zachary. She lay there like Thanksgiving dinner, arms across her chest and legs pulled up to her stomach.

"Great choice. Tell the chef I approved."

The waitress nodded, turned and left the room.

"Gentlemen, dinner is served." Zachary spread her legs, placed his thumbs on her lips and opened them, revealing her clit. "It would seem that chef did not fully prepare our meal, it's not quite moist enough. Let me see what I can do…"

He leaned in and began licking. The other men took turns grabbing her breasts and tweaking her nipples; one taking his fingers and putting them in her mouth. Within moments, she began moaning with delight.

Zachary slid his fingers into her vagina, placed them against her g-spot and began sucking her clit. She began screaming and writhing. The other men pinched and twisted her nipples, attempting to take her over the top. Zachary stopped sucking and bit the engorged nub. Her head came off the table as she let out a loud cacophony and sprayed her juices onto the table.

"I think she is ready," Zachary said as he stood. He dropped his pants, exposing his hard cock. He pulled her to the end of the table and stuck his dick in her. "Ah, yes, perfect temperature. Please, join me in the feast."

The men stood, dropping their pants to the floor. One by one they placed their penises in her mouth or hands. The odd man out was forced to stroke his own as he grabbed her tits.

When Zachary was ready to blow his load, he pulled out of her cunt, grabbed her hair, forcing her into a seated position before he sat in his chair, pulling her with him and placing his rod in her mouth. He pumped her head up and down his shaft, then held her in place as he blew his load down her throat.

She sucked every last drop of cum from his lizard, pulled away and gave him a sex-drunken smile. Their eyes locked as she stood, then wiggled back on the table.

The four men began ravaging her body. One pulled her off the table and instructed her to straddle the man on the floor. She lowered herself on his cock, resting her body on her arms. The man that had extracted her pushed on her lower back, lifting her ass. He lined his head with her brown hole and pushed. The men began pumping her feverishly. The remaining men knelt and began placing their dicks in her face.

"Stephanie, wake up," Maggie nudged her as she spoke.

"What, I'm awake," Stephanie said groggily.

"You were moaning in your sleep. I didn't want anyone else to hear you. It must have been one hell of a dream."

"It was actually quite odd. I think I must be hungry because in my dream I was served up like a turkey."

Maggie shook her head as she laughed. "Only you can come up with this shit."

"I can't help it. It just comes to me."

"It's amazing that you can be so normal the way this crap runs through your head."

"I just think it, I don't act on it. I do have some restraint." Stephanie said with a hint of attitude.

"Thank god! I could not deal with you otherwise."

The ladies relaxed in their seats as the pilot announced they were getting ready for the approach. Stephanie used the time to reflect on the trip. Her thoughts went to Daniel and Zachary; both had been out of character this weekend. Zachary had been the perfect gentleman, not that it was unusual, but the fact that he didn't touch her and left without as much as a good-bye – that was troublesome. Had she done something wrong? Would this interfere with the advertising deal?

Then there was Daniel being so quiet all weekend. Yes, he might have been busy at work, but he normally could find a few moments to shoot a quick text. What, or who, had kept him occupied this whole time? She wouldn't allow her mind think about a "who," there had been no mention and he had been so busy training new people, there could be no way his inattention was due to another woman, he had been doing housework.

The plane landed smoothly. They exited the cabin and walked through the terminal. It was late, and the airport was like a ghost town.

Stephanie was glad she had gotten a cat nap on the plane. The shops were closed, and she would not have been able to grab a coffee for the ride home. They headed to the car and began the drive home.

The ride was quiet. They were both extremely exhausted and grateful that there would be a break next weekend. Yes, Stephanie had to take Brianna to a college, but that would be a walk in the park compared to these trips. Hopefully she would be able to see Daniel and work out some stress.

They pulled into Maggie's driveway. "Are you okay to drive

home?"

"Yes, I'm fine. The nap did me well."

They hugged. Stephanie waited for Maggie to be safely in her house before backing out of the driveway and continuing home to her warm, cozy bed.

She tried not to think about another woman as she drove, but the demon on her shoulder was persistent. It took everything inside her to make him shut up. She was not going to do this. Everything was fine; she was not going looking for trouble.

She pulled in the garage. She grabbed only her purse and headed inside. She opened Brianna's door to make sure she was okay, then headed to her room.

She plugged her phone into the charger and sent two texts, one to Daniel, then to Zachary letting them know she had arrived safely at home. She went to the bathroom to get ready for bed.

She was so tired. She had to push herself through her nightly routine. She would have loved to just collapse in her bed, but she knew that would not be in her best interest. At her age, she really did not need to wake up tomorrow with a big zit on her chin, or worse yet, her nose.

She pulled back the covers as her phone dinged. It was Zachary.

I'm glad you made it home safely. You have had a tough schedule recently, it will be good for you to take some time off. You deserve it.

Stephanie:

Thank you! It will be nice to have some quiet time.

Zachary:

Good night, sleep well.

Stephanie:

Good night

She crawled into bed, pulled up the covers and fell fast to sleep.

CHAPTER 20

"MOM, DID YOU GET me those tights I asked for?" Stephanie awoke in a fog. She did not set an alarm last night and apparently needed sleep. It took a moment for her brain to engage. She groggily said, "Yes, I got them before I left. I thought I put them on the kitchen table."

"Can you go look? I don't remember seeing them and it is freezing."

"Give me a minute." Stephanie opened her eyes wide and stretched her legs. She threw the covers off and got out of bed. She slid into her slippers and headed down the stairs.

She turned the corner and headed into the kitchen. Lo and behold, there was the bag, in plain sight, just as she left it Friday afternoon. She took it off the table and went back up the stairs to Brianna's room.

"It was exactly where I said it would be. Were you not in the kitchen all weekend?"

"I walked through it a couple of times, but I didn't eat there."

"What are you going to do next year when I'm not with you?"

"I guess I'll learn to do things on my own, kind of like I do when you are gone every weekend."

"I see. You can do it, but when mom's around it's just easier to have her do it for you."

"Of course."

Brianna walked past her mom, down the stairs and out the door. Josie was in the driveway waiting for her. A second later, she came back in the house, remembering that she had forgotten her jacket.

Stephanie was at the top of the stairs. "Have a good day."

"See you tonight."

With that the door slammed, and she was gone. Stephanie walked into her bedroom. She looked at her bed; it was calling her to return. She didn't have an appointment until noon, maybe just a few minutes.

She crawled back in and snuggled under the covers. As she was lying there, she began to think about the weekend. Realizing that Daniel had not responded to her text last night, she picked up her phone. Maybe he had after she fell asleep, since that was almost instant.

She pushed her home button, notifications, but no text from Daniel. This was so odd. She knew he would be awake by now, so even if he had been asleep last night, surely he would have messaged her this morning. She put her phone down and closed her eyes, maybe a little cat nap before starting the day.

Although she closed her eyes, she did not sleep. She became bored and decided to just get ready for her day. While she was in her closet, the familiar sound trumpeted through her room.

"It's about fucking time," she thought. She walked over to the nightstand and looked at her phone.

Good morning gorgeous… your kisses put me fast asleep last night and those lips on my cock this morning were a delight.

How could she be upset? It was late when she got in and they had talked before she boarded the plane.

Good morning, handsome! What is a girl to do when she wakes up next to a hard, thick, gorgeous cock? I didn't want to wake you, but I couldn't help myself, I had to take him between my lips and show him how much I adore him.

Daniel:

Oh baby, never apologize for waking me that way. Can't think of a better way to greet the day!

Stephanie:

It will always be my favorite way. Straddling you first thing is a close second, I must admit.

Daniel:

Which ever way you want, works for me. What should I do if I wake before you?

Stephanie:

I love to feel your hard cock against my ass. Kissing my neck, sliding your hand between my thighs, all wonderful first thing in the morning… or anytime.

Daniel:

Bring your ass up here and let me finger that clit while you suck my cock.

Stephanie:

On my knees now. Moving close to you without missing a stroke of that wonderful manhood.

Daniel:

Always thinking of him. Your clit is hard, you must have been dreaming of him.

Stephanie:

Could there be anything else? My mind is filled with ways to please him. It's all I want to do.

Daniel:

Nice… your pussy is wet, sit on top of him.

Stephanie:

Straddling him now. Lining him up just right, slowly lowering onto him. Let me move my lips and get every last inch.

Daniel:

That's it baby, get all of him. Let him spread you wide.

Stephanie:

He is so filling. Leaning forward to start riding. Put your hands on my hips and set the tempo.

Daniel:

Holding your hips and thrusting my cock into your pussy. Feel it deep inside you.

Stephanie:

Feels wonderful! I need to cum. I can't hold back.

Daniel:

Don't hold back. Let it go, soak my balls.

Stephanie:

Letting go. I can't stop cumming. Your balls must be dripping.

Daniel:

It's running down my crack. Do you feel the spray as I pound your cunt?

Stephanie:

I do. I want to feel you explode inside me.

Daniel:

Are you ready?

Stephanie:

Yes I am.

Daniel:

Pushing deep into you, pulling your hips to my groin. Fuuuuccccckkkkk!

Stephanie:

Mmmmm, felt that explosion through my body. Squeezing to hold it in.

Daniel:

Roll over onto the bed. I need to grab a shower. Have a great day!

Stephanie:

Thanks, baby!

Well, that answered the question for her, he had been asleep last night. He must have had a lot of things going on over the weekend to keep him from reaching out. All was well. She went back to her closet and picked out her clothes.

She would take her time showering and doing her make-up. She was beginning to feel the results of burning the candle at both ends. She was mentally and emotionally drained.

She was about to put on her pants, but decided to go with her robe instead. She went downstairs and began boiling a pot of water for tea. There was no reason to be in much before her noon meeting, so she was just going to veg for a couple of hours.

She made her tea and went into the living room to watch television. She needed to let her brain rest.

Nearly an hour into her mindless activity, her phone received a text from her favorite man.

Gorgeous, my schedule is open Thursday evening. What time would work for you?

He remembered.

Will six work for you? It would give me time to head home and change before coming over.
Daniel:
That would be perfect. We can have a drink and then enjoy each other for dinner.
Stephanie:
That would be perfect!
Daniel:
Yes it will. Have a great day!
Stephanie:
You too!

She was reinvigorated. She had Thursday to look forward to now. She decided to go upstairs and get ready; she would head to the coffee shop for a bite to eat before arriving at the office.

While she was in the shower, she thought about how her life was finally falling into place. Brianna was getting ready to head to college, one of her choosing, no doubt, her career was becoming everything she had expected, and things with Daniel were headed into the home stretch. This time next year, she would be able to devote more time to Daniel and her writing with Brianna in school. A great year was just around the corner.

She took a little more time today with her makeup. She would never head to the office without looking good, today she stepped it up a notch; somewhere between a day at work and a date with Daniel.

When she arrived at the coffee shop, there were a few regulars that she saw often. She nodded and gave her good mornings to them all. She then sat in the corner and nibbled on her scone as she watched customers come in and out. She enjoyed watching others and trying to figure out their stories.

An older, well dressed gentleman came in with a young woman, probably 30 years his junior. Stephanie watched as he bought her a latte and they picked a table for two. The young lady sat straight in the chair as the man casually sat in his. Was this a job interview or was he looking for a little toy?

Stephanie continued to watch them from across the room.

She could not hear the conversation. The female pulled some papers out of her large bag and slid them to him. He looked them over quickly and shook her hand across the table. Did she hand him a resume, or was it a contract...

Stephanie watched as they left the café. It was down to the hand placement. If he touched her ass, it was a contract; if he shook her hand—job offer. They walked out the door and shook hands on the other side.

Well that was all to do about nothing, very anticlimactic, like most encounters with men. But in her mind, she could spin it into a tale of fantasy and intrigue. Was that a gift, or a curse?

She glanced at her phone to check the time. Still 45 minutes before her appointment. She saw there was a message from Zachary.

Good morning! I know you are going college shopping with Brianna this week, Mark wanted to set up a photo shoot this month and needs to know your availability.

Stephanie opened her calendar and checked the next few weeks.

Good morning! This week is definitely out. I have a couple of appointments scheduled for next week. I can move them, if necessary, but the following week is open. I am guessing you would want this to happen during the week and not on a weekend, correct?

Zachary:

The photographer will do whatever I tell him. Let me talk it over with Mark and let you know later today before you schedule anything else.

Stephanie:

I will block out that week and let my assistant know when I get to the office.

Zachary:

Ah, living the life of leisure today.

Stephanie:

I wish. My first appointment is at noon, so I'm just taking it slow. Grabbing coffee now and heading to the office in a minute.

Zachary:

Well one day that wish will come true. One day very soon. Enjoy your

day!
    Stephanie:
    Thank you!
Stephanie put the phone in her purse, refilled her cup and headed out the door. She was only minutes away from the office. Everything was prepared for the clients. Maybe she would light some candles, or would that just be over the top? Hmmm…

♦

She had forgone the candles at the office. Her meeting went extremely well, as did the rest of her day. She sent the email to her assistant and they decided to both take that week off and prepare for the holidays, neither one of them had taken the time to begin decorating, or shopping, so this was the perfect excuse, even if Stephanie did not fly to LA for a few days. Certainly just spending a week with Brianna would not be a bad thing.

When Stephanie returned home, Brianna was in the kitchen beginning to prepare supper.

"Well, this is a nice surprise. What are you making?"

"It has been a long time since you have made your chicken and rice, so I decided to start it."

"Just "start" it… in the hopes that I would finish it."

"Yup, I was watching you on the app and saw when you left the office. I didn't want to start too soon."

Stephanie had put her things down and taken off her jacket. She walked over to the sink and washed her hands. "I will finish, but you are going to help. I'm sure your roommates will appreciate you cooking for them."

"They don't have kitchens in the dorms. I will have a meal plan."

"At some point you may want to live off campus and get an apartment."

"Not something I'm in a hurry to do. Then I would have to clean."

"You are going to have to clean your dorm room, there is no

housekeeping."

"That's only one room."

"You just have an answer for everything."

"Yup."

"I'd better see that in your grades."

"Ugh, I don't need that pressure."

"You need to do your best. You don't want to wake up one day and think about what could have been."

"Yeah, yeah, yeah. Do you want to hear what happened today?"

"I don't know… do I want to know?"

"Yes, Josie told me her dad got engaged."

"What?! I didn't even know he was dating anyone. He hasn't been divorced very long."

"He met this woman a couple of months ago and now he's going to marry her."

"Wow, that… is a little nuts. Out of the frying pan and into the fire. How does Josie feel about that?"

"I guess she's okay with it. She likes the woman. Even if she didn't, she's going to college and won't have to live with them."

"Well, she still has to come home during break."

"Yes, but she also has her mother's house as an option."

"True, well I wish them luck."

"Are you sure about that?"

A confused look came over Stephanie's face. "Why wouldn't I?"

"Because you like him."

"He's a nice man, but I wouldn't date him. He's a bit tame for my liking."

"Mom! Do you always have to go there?"

"What did I say?!? There is nothing wrong with my saying he's not my type."

Brianna was now walking out of the kitchen, "That's not what you said. You were too descriptive."

"Hey, where are you going? This isn't finished."

Brianna was headed up the stairs, "There's nothing for me to do. I'm going to my room, you can call me when it's ready."

Stephanie shook her head. Brianna could be such a brat, but she was a good kid. As she stood by the stove stirring her dinner, Stephanie remembered that Zachary had told her he would get back to her today. She pulled her phone out of her purse and checked to see if she missed his message.

She had not missed a message, from anyone. She would message him later this evening, as he did not exactly keep normal business hours.

Stephanie and Brianna had a nice dinner. Brianna had "important homework" to complete, leaving Stephanie alone with the clean up.

With everything put away and the dishes finished, Stephanie went up to her room to throw on some sweats. She had no plans to go anywhere, and after that meal, she needed something a little more forgiving.

Heading back down the stairs, she thought about the last time she had written a story. It had been months. She had been so busy with everything else, she put her writing aside. She decided to go into her office and write something; a blog, short story, poem, just anything to make sure she still had it.

She sat in front of the computer and waited for an idea to come to her... and she waited... and waited a little more. Then it came to her, a story about the couple she had seen earlier today.

She began writing feverishly. She used many of the elements she had observed today, with the exception of the ending. In this story, he placed his hand on her ass and grabbed a handful of butt, showing everyone that cared to watch, who was in charge.

She wrote for an hour or more before the sound of a text grabbed her attention.

Good evening beautiful! Hope you had a great meeting. I had a hard time getting a hold of Mark today; he apparently had meetings out of town. He said that week would be perfect and asked if you could fly in on Tuesday and shoot Wednesday, possibly Thursday, before heading home that evening.

Stephanie:

Good evening! Yes I can do that. My assistant and I decided to take that week off even if I wasn't heading out of town.

Zachary:

Did you tell her what you will be doing?

Stephanie:

LOL, no. I just told her that I might want to get away for a couple of days that week.

Zachary:

Good cover. Will you continue the practice when Debra can pay all the bills?

Stephanie thought about that for a moment.

I think so, but it is going to depend on how time consuming it is. I have to do what is best for myself and my clients. I would prefer to go out on top and not because I was making mistakes or became unreliable.

Zachary:

Good way to look at it. Glad you are thinking ahead. How are things going with Dan now that you are not as available?

Stephanie:

Everything is going really well! I am going to see him Thursday before I head away for the weekend. I am looking forward to it, since it has been quite some time.

Zachary:

I see, so others have been taking care of you.

Stephanie:

If "others" means inanimate objects with batteries and cords, yes, you are correct.

Zachary:

That is too bad. Does he know you have not been seeing anyone else?

Stephanie:

I think he does. I haven't been telling him any stories about other men and he asked about you.

Zachary:

What did you tell him about me?

Stephanie:

I told him that you were the perfect gentleman and since we had taken

things to another level, you and I didn't do anything.
Zachary:
How did he react?
Stephanie:
He was very surprised. I guess he assumed that you would just continue.
Zachary:
We are different that way.
Stephanie:
?
Zachary:
I have boundaries I won't cross.
Stephanie:
Are you saying he doesn't?
Zachary:
I am saying we are different, that is all, nothing more.
Stephanie:
Well that's the way it came across.
Zachary:
I was making a statement based on myself. I need to head to a party. Good night.
Stephanie:
Good night.

Stephanie thought it odd that Zachary would react as he did. Could he be jealous? There was no reason for that, he was planning to stay single; you can't want to be single and jealous at the same time. Men. She would never understand them.

The writing had worn her out. She headed upstairs to get ready for bed. Tomorrow things would be back to a regular schedule, she wanted to be sure she was rested.

She was almost asleep when she got a text from Daniel.

Good evening, gorgeous! How are the twins tonight? Are those nipples hard?

Fuck! Why couldn't he have done this an hour ago? She rolled onto her side and picked up her phone.

Good evening, handsome. The twins are nice and cozy snuggling in bed with me.

Daniel:

Rub those nipples as you snuggle with them. Let me crawl in next to you and bite each one.

Yeah, apparently he didn't get the hint that she was ready to sleep. She would continue the banter, but he had better keep up on his part or she just might nod off on him.

Let me roll onto my back and give you access. I will run my fingers through your hair as you bite hard and make me cum.

Daniel:

Rubbing your clit as I bite. So juicy, let's get through the first one so I can fuck you.

Stephanie:

My, my, you are a bit anxious. What has you so worked up?

Daniel:

It has been a while since I've had you. Thursday can't get here soon enough.

Stephanie:

I know, baby. I want you more than you can imagine. I need to feel you. I need to feel our energy. I miss you terribly.

Daniel:

I know, honey. Before you know it you will be in my arms again. Let's plan lots of kissing before moving to other things.

Stephanie:

We can plan, but you know how it goes.

Daniel:

LOL the motors do get heated up very quickly and it's off to the races.

Stephanie:

Yes, zero to a million in a moment.

Daniel:

We do have amazing chemistry.

Stephanie:

That's hard to find.

Daniel:

Agreed. Night night sexy.

Stephanie:

Good night, handsome.

They did have an amazing chemistry. What she felt with him she had never felt before. It was the thing that kept her going. She didn't ever want to lose it. She fell asleep with the warm feelings of their deepening relationship.

CHAPTER 21

S HE WAS UP before the alarm. The past two days had drawn on, but today she would be meeting her man. She would be spending a wonderful evening in his arms. She was like a giddy schoolgirl going on her first date.

As she picked out what she would wear for work, she put together another outfit for her evening with Daniel. She planned to work until four, then drive home, shower and dress, maybe grab a nibble, before heading to his house. She had no meetings planned, so getting out on time should not be an issue.

She had showered and was getting dressed when she got her first message.

Good morning, gorgeous! Today is the day! Are you ready?
Stephanie:
Good morning, handsome! I was ready last week, I don't even know what to call what I am now.
Daniel:
LOL tonight will be wonderful. I grabbed a bottle of your favorite wine. I promise we will have a glass before anything happens.
Stephanie:
Well that means you can't kiss me at the door. You know that starts the engines.
Daniel:
Hey! I can control myself when necessary.
Stephanie:
I know you can. You are going to have to think about me as a client.
Daniel:
I don't think we need to go that far. I will just pretend we are in public.
Stephanie:
That sounds like a good plan.

Daniel:
I have an early meeting, have a great day!
Stephanie:
I will because I know it will be topped off with you.
Daniel:
Thank you sexy!
Stephanie:
You're welcome, handsome!

She finished getting ready and quickly headed to the office, she couldn't wait to get this part of her day into the books and get to her date.

For the most part, the day went as expected. There were a couple of off the wall calls from clients, but otherwise, it was business as usual. Stephanie decided to take her assistant out to lunch and see if she was happy with things as they were or if she might want to get more involved which would allow Stephanie more time at home to write. Her hope was a three or four-day week. If her assistant was willing to be fulltime, it could happen, the only other option was to hire a second assistant. At this time, that would not be possible. She did not have the time to train someone.

They went to a local diner. The hostess seated them in a quiet, corner booth. There was the typical small talk, the real conversation didn't begin until they had placed their lunch order.

"As you know, I have been working on another project."

"Yes, that's the reason you have been out of the office the past few Fridays."

"Correct. Things have been going very well with the project. I expect that it will consume more of my time in the coming year."

Stephanie sensed a bit of worry on Pam's face.

"Don't worry, you are not going to lose your job. As a matter of fact, I asked you to come to lunch to discuss you heading toward a full-time position. I would eventually like to only work three or four days a week. If you were able to be in the office

Monday through Friday, you can handle the day to day things and I will just need to work on the big stuff.

I would always be available for phone calls in case of emergency, but I really want more time with Brianna and this project."

"Do I need to give you an answer right now?"

"No, of course you don't. I understand you need time to think about it and talk with your husband. This is not something that will happen next week. This is something that is months down the road. I just want to be prepared when the time gets here."

"Okay, that's a relief. I'm not sure how my husband would feel about me being out of the house every day. The children are getting older, but we don't like them to come home to an empty house."

"I completely understand. I started the business so I had flexibility when Brianna was small. You could bring the children to the office after school, or have the bus drop them off. It would give them dedicated time to do homework."

"I will talk that over with him as well. More than likely we can work something out."

"I hope we can, our only other option would be to hire another part timer, or not overlapping our time together. After you talk to your husband, we will meet again and brainstorm about the path forward." Stephanie had a thought shoot into her mind. "You might also want to talk to your husband about one day taking over the business."

Pam was surprised with the thought. "I never dreamed of owning a business. That is not something I am familiar with and I know I'm not ready."

Stephanie chuckled, "I'm not talking about that happening tomorrow. It's just a fact that one day I will want to retire. I don't plan on doing this forever. I've hit 50 and I don't want to do this another 15 years."

"Well, I hope you want to do it for at least another three or four."

As the ladies were laughing, their food was brought to the table. They began talking about kids and mundane things. They finished and headed back to the office.

The afternoon went quickly. Before she knew it, it was time to close up and head home. Pam had left an hour ago She seemed pleased with the opportunities that Stephanie had posed. It looked like things were looking up for everyone.

Her phone vibrated.

Good afternoon gorgeous! And the countdown begins... two hours to your lips on mine.

Stephanie became even more excited.

Hello, handsome! Yes, I have been counting down since this morning. I can't wait to be in your arms. I miss you.

Daniel:

I know it has been too long. I will work on that.

Stephanie:

I can't wait to have a normal schedule again. I need to have my lips wrapped around your cock more often.

Daniel:

He would love that! My lips would fight him and expect them first.

Stephanie:

We have enough time for both. I'm not going anywhere.

Daniel:

I know we do.

Stephanie:

Let me get going, I need to get ready for you.

Daniel:

I'm sure you are perfect as you are.

Stephanie:

Thank you, handsome!

Daniel:

You're welcome sexy!

She grabbed her things from the desk and placed them in her purse. She put on her coat as she turned off the lights, grabbing her bag from the desk as she headed toward the door.

She had forgotten to start the car, but it wasn't too bad, she

Question of Trust

could handle a little cold on the drive, besides, her thoughts would keep her warm. She drove quicker than normal, the anticipation heavy on her mind.

She pulled in the garage. The door had not reached the floor and Stephanie was in the house and headed up the stairs. Brianna had plans for this evening with her friends, so there would be no distraction.

Her clothes were on the counter in the bathroom. It took a few moments for the water in the shower to turn warm, but as soon as it did, she was in it and washing her body. She focused on her goal, trying not to get distracted, as she had a tendency to do.

She dried off, dressed and dried her hair. She slowed down when she got to her makeup. She wanted to look like she was going on a date, not just coming from the office. She took extra time to detail her eyes and lips, her best features.

She took a look in the mirror, damn she looked good. She hoped he would think the same. She had chosen pants and a form fitting sweater, every curve shown through. She wore heels and picked out chunky earrings and a necklace to complete her look.

She took a deep breath and headed back to her car. She had butterflies for the first time in years. She could not stop smiling as she got into her car and headed to Daniel.

While driving, she began thinking about all the wonderful things that had happened between them recently. Her mind focused on the weekend at the cabin. It had been weeks since that time, but it seemed like yesterday. Now that her traveling schedule was easing, she was looking forward to many more of those weekends.

She imagined the ones in the summer would be spent scantily clad, possibly naked. Maybe those men would get used to them fucking on the rock and not even take notice. Although, Daniel might get upset if they were to just walk by and not acknowledge his skill in the pleasure department.

In no time she was pulling into Daniel's driveway. She took

165

a quick look in the mirror to be sure she still looked flawless. She smiled at her reflection, grabbed her purse off the seat next to her, and headed toward the front door.

The inside door was ajar, but Stephanie knocked anyway. She was not comfortable just walking in, even though she knew that's what he wanted her to do.

Daniel pulled open the inside door and she opened the storm door. He greeted her with a kiss. Not a deep kiss, but one that was just enough to know that he missed her without getting the motors running. He was sticking to his word; they would enjoy a drink, spoon a bit, and then get to business.

He took her by the hand and walked her into the living room. They sat on the sofa next to each other, but facing.

"So tell me, you've done signings and conventions, have you seen an uptick in business."

"Yes, we have. Maggie has been tracking it closely. We decided in the beginning what we were looking for in terms of numbers and agreed that if we were not getting the results we would discontinue, regroup, and then take another path. I did not want to waste time and money on something that was not beneficial."

"Very good, I assumed that was the case, but I thought I would clarify. Now this weekend is to look at a college for Brianna, correct?"

"Yes. This would be the one that is at the top of her list. It is one of the top schools in her area of study, so of course the price tag reflects that. She is going to have to get student loans and scholarships. Debra does not make that kind of income... yet."

They both chuckled.

"There is nothing wrong with her having some skin in the game. I think it helps them do better when they have something to lose."

"I'm sure it does. I didn't get a free ride. I had to work and get student loans to get through school. I can help her more than my parents were able to help me, but she needs responsibility."

"I see it in hiring new employees, the ones that had more skin in the game always outperform the silver spoons." Daniel sat forward on the sofa. Stephanie thought he was about to make the move to spooning, but she was wrong. "You know, there is something missing. I forgot to get us drinks to toast your success. Let me go grab your wine. Do you mind if I have a Jack and Coke?"

"That's fine. You have your favorite, I have mine."

"Okay, wait right here and I will return with drinks and maybe a little snack. I haven't gotten to the store this week, so the cupboards are a bit bare. Just give me a few minutes, doll. Sit back and relax."

He gave her a kiss and left the room. Stephanie sat back on the sofa and felt the warm feelings for him well up inside her. He was such a wonderful man. She felt like the luckiest woman in the world.

As she sat there, she kept hearing a vibrating noise that was nearly non-stop. Daniel had left his phone on the table, face up. She went to grab it and take it to him thinking something important was going on, but her eyes caught a glimpse of a text.

Can't wait to repeat our weekend at the cabin! You are beyond the best lover I have ever had.

Stephanie's heart stopped. Yes, the rules were he was able to see other women, but she didn't really believe he had been doing it. "Their weekend at the cabin." He had taken another woman to the place that she was told was theirs.

Her mind was racing. At this moment everything she had thought was reality had been shattered. The closeness that she thought had grown... was just a figment of her imagination. She had been warned this would happen, but she didn't believe anyone. Could she really have been taken for such a ride? How could she have been so wrong?

Daniel came in with glasses in his hand, one of them balancing a plate of miscellaneous foods. When he saw her face, he knew something was wrong. He quickly put everything down and sat next to her.

"What happened? Is everything alright?"

She was calm, she had no emotion, her eyes were hollow. "I'm sorry. Your phone was vibrating off the hook. I thought something was wrong. I was going to grab it and bring it to you. It was facing up—I couldn't help but see the message."

Daniel could not imagine what had caused this distress. He picked up his phone and saw what she had read.

"Oh, honey, that's just some crazy nut that I ran into when I went to the cabin weeks ago."

Stephanie looked deflated. "She said you spent the weekend with her in the cabin. I thought I was the only one you would have there."

Daniel tried to be jovial, "Baby, you are the only one I have in *my* cabin. She has her own place. It was nothing."

Stephanie felt as though she was in a nightmare. She could barely breathe. She sat motionless and emotionless. "You had not mentioned anyone else, so this is surprising."

He began to get a bit defensive, "A gentleman doesn't kiss and tell. You have other men—you should understand that I have other women."

The haze in Stephanie's head began to clear. "How many others are there?"

"That doesn't matter. You are the one I care about most."

Stephanie wanted to cry, but the tears didn't come. She was still in shock. A piece of her took comfort in being told that she was number one, but the remainder was shattered. The sliver of her heart that remained grasped onto those words and held it with everything imaginable.

She began to calm. They were quiet for a few moments. She needed to process things in her mind. It didn't feel real. Maybe it wasn't real. Maybe he had set this whole thing up. It was convenient that the other woman had begun her texts when he was out of the room. This could just be a test to see if she really was okay with him seeing other women. Yes, that had to be it, there was no other explanation. She held tightly to that belief as she took a deep breath and found the strength to muster a smile.

"I just want to be number one. None of the others can be

above me."

"They can't hold a candle to you. Now how about we continue where we left off?"

Daniel took the plate off the one glass, grabbed both cups, then handed one to Stephanie. He touched his drink to hers as he said, "Here's to a beautiful, talented, gorgeous woman. I wish you more continued success in the future."

They sipped their libations for a bit as he held her hand. The alcohol helped numb her feelings. She took his hand to hers lips and kissed it. He hadn't lost her. She was still in love with him.

He took her glass and placed both on the table. He leaned in and gently began kissing her. He placed his hand on her cheek and looked into her eyes. They were empty. He knew he had work to do. He began slowly kissing her cheeks, then down her neck.

At first, she didn't respond. She wasn't sure she was ready to do this. Her mind kept telling her that she knew the rules, but her heart felt betrayed. She struggled to make sense of it all.

He continued to place pecks on her neck. He placed a hand on her breast, his thumb in search of a hard nipple. Not finding one, he grabbed the flesh harder, pawing it until he received his desired result – she was becoming stimulated, he still had a chance.

The struggle inside persisted for her as he continued. She did still love him, and she knew this could happen one day. He said he wanted her the most. If she was number one, did it matter there were others who weren't? If she had his heart, did it matter that they occasionally got his dick?

No, it didn't matter, she wanted his heart. This was the man she loved, and she was not going to give him to another woman. She put the hurt away and gave in to her lust for him.

She put her hands on the sides of his face and brought his lips to hers. She kissed him passionately. He knew he had won her over. He pulled back and looked into her eyes, they were beginning to sparkle once again.

He stood and reached his hand out to her, she took it. He

pulled her up from the sofa and led her through the living room and up the stairs into the "play" room.

He walked her next to the bed, then turned toward her, putting his hands through her hair, and driving his tongue into her mouth. His fingers tightened on her long locks. He pulled her head back to nibble her neck.

She let out a little moan as he grabbed her tit and began mauling it. He placed his hand under her shirt in search of the nipple. He pulled the breast out of its holder, pushed up her shirt and took the protruding flesh into his mouth. He sucked it for a few moments before giving it a firm bite.

She gasped and gave out a little squeal, letting him know he had gotten a little rough.

He looked at her while rubbing the sore nipple. He placed his other hand under the shirt and lifted it over her head and dropped it to the floor. He kissed her lightly as he reached around her and unhooked her bra.

He stepped back from her, dragging his hands up her back, hooking his fingers in her bra, pulling it forward, releasing her boobs, then letting it fall to the ground.

Her hands began to move toward him, but he shook his head – no. He took off his clothes as she stood by the bed, waiting.

She scanned every inch of his body. Were there parts she liked? Were there parts she didn't like? Was this really the man she wanted to be with forever? So many questions running through her mind, they just would not stop.

He took her by the shoulders and nudged her onto the bed. As she lay across the bed, he loosened her pants, slid them off, and threw them with her top. He moved her panties to the side and began rubbing her clit with his thumb.

She wanted to feel the excitement, but she couldn't. She tried to focus on the manipulation, but her mind was racing. Does he do this to her? Is this her favorite? I prefer his fingers in my pussy, did he confuse us?

Realizing he wasn't getting the expected result, he took off her underwear and began licking between her lips. He added some sucking and nibbling before placing two fingers deep inside her.

She began to enjoy his fingers. Her mind quieted just enough for her to get moist. She was far from her usual dripping self when he lined up his cock and pushed it into her hole.

He placed her legs on his shoulders, grabbed her hips, and began pounding deep into her cunt. He tried manipulating her little man in the boat in order to have her orgasm. It didn't work. He pulled his dick from her.

"Get on all fours, I want you from behind."

She crawled into the middle of the mattress and assumed the position. He needed to spit on his penis, as she was not a wet mess like she should have been by now. No worries, this position always made her cum.

He did his best to stimulate her, but her head was not in the game. She didn't want to disappoint him, so she finally began moaning as she does when having an orgasm.

"Yes, baby, just like that. Keep going, I'm ready to cum."

"Keep going sexy, get over that hump, let your juices flow. Shall I combine mine with yours, or would you prefer them elsewhere?"

Right now there was no way she could possibly swallow a load, "I want them deep inside me, mixing with mine."

Really they would not be mixing with hers because she didn't have any to give him. She just couldn't; this felt more like a chore than any type of pleasure. Was this the way it was going to be in the future? She certainly hoped it wouldn't, she needed his sex to escape reality. She was sure it would be better next time—after she could process things in her own mind.

She left out a scream, partly to fake the orgasm, but also because it was beginning to hurt, she had never been so dry with him before.

"There we go, that's better. Get ready sexy, here... it... comes..."

She could feel him explode inside her. It was a relief, but not in the way it normally was. This time it was more of a – thank god it's over – type of relief.

He flopped onto the bed next to her and pulled her close. "You were not really into this tonight. I'm sure we will be back to normal next time."

"I'm sorry, my mind wouldn't shut up."

"It's okay, there was a lot to process. I hate upsetting my favorite lady."

She held him tighter and snuggled into him more. She had always told herself she just wanted to be number one and he was telling her that was her place. She should be satisfied with it, but was she?

They lay next to each other for another ten minutes before she moved to get up and use the bathroom. When she returned, he had begun to get dressed. She picked up her clothes, putting them on as she did.

They spoke very little. He walked her down the stairs, where she grabbed her purse and headed to the door.

"Can I get you a drink? Water? Soda? Another glass of wine? Something stronger?"

"No thank you, I still have quite a bit to do. I have not packed. There are a few emails I need to send. I really just need to get home."

He hugged her tight and kissed the top of her head. "Alright, I'll let you go. Have a safe trip. I hope Brianna likes the school."

"I'm sure she will. It is her favorite."

"Hopefully, reality will be just as good as her mental image."

"Yes, let's hope so," she kissed his lips and headed out the door. He was watching as she walked to the car and backed out of the driveway.

She did not get far down the street before breaking out in tears. She had thought there was no one else. He had told her he was busy with meetings and social obligations. He must have been lying to her the entire time. Should she believe that the woman was not in *their* cabin?

She began to think about all the clues she had missed. She remembered him telling her that she did not need to mark the cabin's location because he would always be with her because there had been bears sighted nearby. WTF?!? Bare women in the bedroom, maybe.

How many times had he gone MIA on weekends that she was away? Did he use it as a – when the cat's away the mice will play—time? Was it someone different every time, or was it just one other woman?

What if it was **one** other woman? That would be the worst. Did she get a key on a heart keychain as well? Did he tell her that she was number one? What would Stephanie believe going forward? What would she believe of the past?

She pulled into her garage still whimpering. She needed to get it together, Brianna could be home. The thought of Brianna seeing her like this, considering she didn't like Daniel, was not something Stephanie could deal with tonight. She took a few deep breaths, wiped her eyes, then checked the rear-view mirror to be sure she was presentable.

She wasn't the best, her eyes were a bit puffy, but the tears had stopped. She could quickly say hello and get upstairs without Brianne noticing. She would just tell her she was tired and wanted to get ready for bed before they talked more. She had her plan, now to execute.

She got out of the car and headed into the house. She said hello, but got no response. She headed up the stairs to check Brianna's bedroom. She wasn't there. This would have been much easier had she checked the app for her location. She just wasn't thinking straight. She went into her bathroom and readied herself for bed.

About five minutes later, Brianna came in the front door. By this time, Stephanie had cleaned up and was packing her bags.

"Hello, did you get everything packed?" Stephanie asked as she heard Brianna coming up the stairs.

"No, I didn't have time."

"Okay, make sure you do it tonight, I don't want to rush in the morning."

"I'm going into my room to do it now. We had a good night."

"That's good. Are any of the girls visiting colleges this weekend?"

"No, they all think they have found their perfect school."

"Well that's good. I hope this one is what you expect."

"Me too." Brianna went into her room.

Stephanie continued to pack. It was only a few days, but she wanted this to be a nice weekend with Brianna. She was planning to take her to a nice restaurant and the beach was not far away, that meant additional clothes. Her packing for three days was more like preparing for a week. She tried to at least combine the most outfits to match with the least amount of shoes.

She placed the suitcase by her bedroom door and crawled into bed with her laptop. She would check emails and send the few she spoke about earlier. It didn't take long to finish. She closed the computer before looking at social media. She was exhausted and needed rest.

She turned off the light and sent a message to Daniel before nodding off.

Honey, thank you. I need to know I am the only one with feelings in this. As long as you are honest with me and they know it's nothing more than a fuck because there is someone else in your life, I'll be okay. I had been very forward with the men I have had in the past. I understand that to you they mean nothing, but they need to know that as well, we are talking about women. They are emotional and attach too quickly. I really don't want any unnecessary bullshit. I want to grow old with you, but can we keep the drama to a minimum? I love you.

She put her phone on the nightstand and rolled over to sleep.

CHAPTER 22

HER ALARM WOKE HER from a deep sleep. She got out of bed and headed for the bathroom. As she was waiting for the water to warm, she walked back to her nightstand and looked at her phone. No message from Daniel. That was odd, but maybe he dozed off as he so often does. She went back to brush her teeth and hop in the shower.

The water felt comforting as it ran down her body. Thoughts of last night came into her mind. She focused on how odd the timing of the text had been. Could this really just be a test to see if she was going to keep to her word? She pushed it out of her mind; there were other things she needed to focus on now.

She dried off and dressed in a casual traveling outfit. She debated full makeup, but since she had to pack it anyway, she used it as she did. Taking the pouch in her hand, she turned off the light and placed the bag in her suitcase.

Brianna's light shown from under the door. Stephanie popped her head in the room just to make sure Brianna was out of bed and getting ready. She was. Stephanie took her satchel to the car and placed it in the trunk, leaving it open for Brianna's luggage.

While she waited for Brianna, Stephanie made herself a cup of coffee. She suddenly realized that she had left her phone upstairs. She went up into her room and retrieved it. Her phone was her life, she couldn't leave it behind.

She had returned to the kitchen and was drinking her coffee, skimming through social media as Brianna walked in.

"I'm ready to go."

"Do you have everything?"

"Yes, I made a list, everything is checked off."

"Okay, let's get your bag in the car and head out."

They went into the garage, loaded the car, and began their road trip. It would be a six-hour drive and Stephanie was pretty sure Brianna would sleep most of the way.

♦

The drive had been uneventful. Brianna took little cat naps, but was awake for most of it, the anxiety must have gotten the better of her.

Stephanie had spoken to the hotel and asked that they be able to check in early. She did not want to head over to the college in her traveling clothes and they needed to register at the college by 2 pm.

They pulled into the hotel at 12:30 pm. The person at the front desk was the one she had spoken to on the phone. Everything went smoothly and by 12:45 pm, they were in their room, giving them plenty of time to freshen up and change.

The short drive to the campus was gorgeous. Tree lined streets with beautiful, well landscaped homes welcomed them to the town. They had used the GPS, but you certainly could not miss the entrance sign.

The parking lot was already packed, this had been touted to be their biggest exposition weekend for incoming freshmen. From the look of things so far, that was an understatement.

Balloons and upper classmen lined the walk into the registration building. They waited 20 minutes in line before receiving their badges and weekend itinerary. They were then whisked into a reception area where they could grab a drink and nibble on the light fare sprinkled around the room.

At the far end, there was a wall of glass, lined with double doors. They could see people leaving and getting onto buses for a tour. They made their way through the room, stopping occasionally to talk to professors and students dressed in outfits distinguishing them as liaisons.

Stephanie got caught up in the excitement of the upcoming

year. They had a wonderful day of touring and questioning. Stephanie could see why this was Brianna's first choice.

It wasn't until later in the day that Stephanie began taking notice to all the couples with their student walking around the campus. She began to feel sad. It wasn't about being a single mom, it was about the love and partnership of the couples.

Yes, of course, for some of them it could just be a show, but the fact was that she wanted what they had. She wanted that person in her life, standing by her, supporting her decisions. Had she been here last weekend, things would have been very different. She would have felt that she had what they had—now she wasn't so sure.

Her mind began playing scenarios of what Daniel might be doing tonight. She was out of town, he had not responded to her message from last night, he must be with another woman.

She tried not to let Brianna know what was going through her mind. She put on the smiles and kept the conversation positive while deep inside, she was dying.

After the tours, Stephanie took Brianna to a little diner before going back to the hotel.

"This is a very nice school. Is it still your first choice?"

"Yes, I don't want to look at any others."

"Okay, then when we get back to the hotel I want you to begin the application process. They don't accept everyone, so let's make sure you are in before we stop touring other colleges."

"They will accept me, it's my fate."

"I have no doubt that they will accept you; let's just get it in writing."

Brianna gave her an eye roll and went back to eating her meal.

While Brianna was filling out her application, Stephanie needed to get some air. She grabbed her briefcase and went out to sit on the patio.

She sat at the small table that was in the corner and way from the other guests. She took out her laptop and checked emails. There were a few that needed to be answered, but it didn't take her long to finish. She placed her computer back in her bag, then sat back and watched as people mulled about.

As far as her demons were concerned, there would be no rest for the weary. They bombarded her with worries and uneasiness. She was unable to relax, there was only one way she could deal with this – she needed to write him a letter.

She dug through her satchel and found a notebook. Not her normal letter writing paper, but it would have to do. She pulled out a pen and began spilling herself onto the paper.

Daniel,

Today was very difficult. Seeing all these couples, and not hearing from you, is driving my demons crazy. I want answers, but all I seem to get are more questions. I know you don't like explanations and you want things to go your way, but I need answers. You have not told me anything about your feelings and plans for the future, even though I have told you mine.

Yes, you did tell me last night that I mean more to you, but how much more? The questions I need answered are these-

The biggest one is, why don't you trust me? I trusted you with my life. I agreed to openness, I took you at your word when you said there were no other women and you would tell me before there was someone.

You said this happened one time, weeks ago. How could you get caught if it was just this one time? Honestly, it almost seems staged.

Did I react wrongly? Was I supposed to get mad at you and leave you so you didn't have to break up with me?

I need to have answers so I can move past this in my mind. I am now going to ask that you give me the answers and trust that I can deal with whatever they are. The ball is in your court.

S

She put the pen away, stood, and placed the bag on her shoulder. She took the papers from the table and folded them. She went to the front desk to see if they had an envelope and a stamp. She addressed the letter and left it with the attendant to place in the mail.

She felt a little relief as she got on the elevator and headed back to the room.

When she walked in, Brianna had finished the application and was snapchatting with her friends. Stephanie asked if everything went okay with the application and Brianna told her she had gotten a confirmation email that told her she would have the decision in two weeks.

Stephanie was mentally exhausted. She got ready for bed even though it was barely nine o'clock. Before she nodded off, she sent a text to Daniel.

Good bye

Not having heard from him since she left his house, she felt as though this was the end. If it was, then she would pick herself up and move on. She was well aware that things did not always go her way, but she became stronger for it.

She had done what she could; now she would rest.

♦

The weekend had gone well. Brianna was satisfied with her choice and the decision met with Stephanie's approval as well. It was late morning before they got on the road. They had many things to discuss and the trip went quickly.

They were about an hour from home when Stephanie stopped at a restaurant for dinner. She did not feel like cooking when they got home.

They were seated quickly and served promptly. In less than an hour, they were back on the road for the final miles home.

The closer they got to the house, the more anxiety began to build up within Stephanie. The last thing she had heard from Daniel was a text saying good night after she had fallen asleep

Friday. She really did not want this to be over, but it seemed as though he had made that decision.

By the time they arrived at home, Stephanie had driven herself into a panic. She fought to keep it hidden from Brianna. She was relieved when Brianna told her she would be going over to Josie's house for a short time to talk about the trip.

Stephanie told Brianna to be careful and then began unpacking. As she did, her mind continued tormenting her. She placed her clothes in the hamper and saw the shirt she had worn over to Daniel's. She began crying hysterically. The cry was the deep, gut wrenching, bowels of hell type of cry. It was uncontrollable and she began to hyperventilate.

She was able to calm down, eventually. She needed answers right now. He must have gotten the letter today. She needed to hear his voice, she called his phone.

It rang, then went to voicemail. He was avoiding her. A couple minutes later, she got a text.

Hey sexy…sorry I missed your call. I had an end of day meeting, just finished nine holes.

Stephanie:

I need you.

Daniel:

I hope you didn't shoot or stab anyone! Lol

Stephanie could not believe how casual he was about everything.

I'm hurting baby.

Daniel:

I'm picking up supper and will call you when I'm home.

Stephanie:

Ok

Stephanie went into the kitchen and made a cup of chamomile tea. She needed something to calm her nerves, but wanted to be sane when Daniel called her. She tried occupying her mind with returning emails and getting ready for clients.

She had finished her tea, yet no phone call. Maybe he was reading the letter and trying to come up with answers before he made the call.

Two hours had gone by since their last message. Stephanie was feeling avoided and had cracked open a bottle of wine.

Are you trying to avoid me or is your ADD really that bad?

Daniel:

Had an emergency meeting with my attorney, the merger isn't going well. Give me five minutes.

Stephanie:

I'm not trying to be flip, you just drive me to drink.

Daniel:

I know… I'm sorry.

Stephanie:

Did you get my letter?

Daniel:

Got my mail, but did not read. Do I need to read it first?

Stephanie:

Might be a good idea.

Daniel:

This may not be a good time then…I have to read and think before I respond. My mood and emotions not tuned into dealing with new stuff. I'm very sorry you are hurting and that I am obviously the source of your pain. Somewhere I missed or ignored that you were taking our relationship way beyond friends, lovers and Master/slave. Hurting you was never my intention. I have never stopped dating as was always my intention. My dates are a total variety of levels. We will talk after I read the letter and gather my thoughts.

Stephanie was now at the edge. What the fuck was he saying? This made no sense to her.

I am confused. You told me there were no others and you would tell me when there was. I have told you exactly how I feel, so I'm confused how you didn't know. Although I guess I should be more concerned about how stupid I was. I really missed this one.

Daniel:

We will talk. I never talked to others about you or you about others. In the beginning, I assumed all of the plans were kidding, dreaming and teasing. Stephanie, I don't think I have an interest in the lifestyle anymore.

I helped you grow into the woman you are and helped you withstand the difficulties. I should have spoke up long ago. I maintained two different lives and time is coming to move back to my professional life.

After seeing Zachary's board room and the dungeon, Stephanie realized that she and Daniel were not "lifestyle," they in fact were not much more than kinky with rough sex. They had only used handcuffs on one occasion and she was not tied to a cross. Although the reading of those words cut her, she knew she had done nothing wrong.

I can completely understand that and I have not done any lifestyle things since my trip to LA. I haven't taken on any new men, either. It's just been you. It's unfortunate that you don't think I could fit into your - professional life. I spent nearly two decades loyal to an emotionally abusive man who didn't have sex with me for over a decade. You did help me grow, but I wish you would have been honest. Not just with me, but with all of them. I don't think the others would have taken it as well. I'm glad you mentioned what song to play at your funeral.

She sent that message and began typing again.

There were many people who told me you were a user, but I thought they didn't understand you. I admit I had the blinders on. Now that I know the truth, I am much better. Just be careful, I don't want to see you hurt any more than you are now. You are playing with fire by not being above board. As you see, it will come out and it won't always go well.

She thought about his life and things he had told her, she continued.

I'm not angry and the pain has subsided. I think not knowing was the worst. I always seem to find these guys that need fixing, but aren't ready to change. I wish I could have helped you as much as you helped me. You are an amazing man and I know from recent conversations you don't believe it. I think you have issues with your father. They were not helped by the fact that you were your mother's favorite. She still loves you so much. She wants the best for you. Not sure how I know that, but I do. Get some sleep, handsome, you need your strength for your meeting tomorrow. I'm still on your side.

It was strange, the calm she felt seemed like it had been a long time coming. She hadn't lashed out at him. She kept her feelings in adult mode, not resorting to name calling and belittling him. Her heart was numb. She had hung so many things on this relationship. She wasn't sure how she would proceed. She felt her safety net was gone.

Daniel, however, was not on that level.

I never understand why it is assumed I am not above board. Our Master/slave is not supposed to be in the open. Our friendship at events we attended, were all open. The slaves know there are other slaves and the dates know there are other dates. The two worlds are not supposed to intersect. I am leaving the Dom world. I enjoy your company and professionalism. It is unbelievable that I am called a user. Women are such users. I am a great lover with a great cock, but no one knows that until there is real chemistry. But I am the one who has walked away when it is only sex. Several women begged me to fuck them on the side…accused me of ruining their sex life…I am certainly not the user. I have never taken advantage of our relationship and been there for you. The public can stop worrying as I consider monogamy and someone closer to my age, enjoys sex, but sees me for more than my cock. You have been more than that, but certainly a focal point.

Night night sexy.

Again, what the fuck was that?!? Someone closer to his own age? Why the fuck would that matter? Seeing him only as a cock? No, that certainly was not the way she viewed him. The braggart side was something she had not witnessed before, and was frankly taken aback by it.

She now had much more to say. If he wanted someone his age, she was going to show him the error of that conclusion.

You are so much more than your cock. Why you want an old woman is beyond me. Who is going to take care of your ass when you get older? Good night.

Daniel:

LMAO…you have a wonderful personality and sense of humor. I will need a nurse? Prop for my cock.

Stephanie:

I am too young for you. I really don't think you could keep up.

Daniel:

LMAO…*then discard me like roadkill.*
Stephanie:
I probably would kill you. You do realize that if your cock were here 24/7 I would take it every time I got horny. Can you go three times a day? But you don't have to worry about that with an old lady. Three times a month will take care of her. I'm sure you can get it up that often.
Daniel:
Thanks for making me smile.
Stephanie:
Daniel, I have told you many times, I only want to make you happy.
There was no response after this message. She crawled into bed and went to sleep.

♦

Her alarm sounded. She had just gotten out of bed when his text came in.
Good morning sexy! I appreciate that and hopefully returned that sentiment as well. Happiness starts internally before externally…have a fabulous day!
Well now what the hell did that mean – internally before externally. Did that mean that you need to have feelings for someone before they can make you happy? Do you need to be happy with yourself first? Why were things never easy?
Good morning, handsome! I hope all goes well in the meeting today. I want to stop by tomorrow night and continue our conversation.
Daniel:
Sorry, I'm not available. I can do Thursday.
Stephanie:
So someone else has my spot. I'll be over on Thursday.
Daniel:
So sarcasm invades…it's a cookout not at my home…oh my gosh and without sex. See you Thursday.
Stephanie:
Relax baby, no sarcasm, just kidding. I guess I need to put in lols or something. Didn't mean to upset you. I'm not like that.

Daniel:

Have a great day!

Stephanie:

Good luck!

She readied herself for work. She wanted to get there early and begin the catch up. She was less than an hour early, not what she had hoped, but to her surprise, there was really nothing to do other than a few emails. Pam had answered any incoming questions and got some client files up to date.

Stephanie was now sure that she had made the right decision by asking Pam to take on more time. Seeing what Pam had done without guidance, Stephanie thought that maybe she should push just a little harder to get "Debra" to take over as the major bread winner and then let Pam take over the business.

Stephanie worked on a few projects until after lunch. She knew Daniel's meeting had been earlier in the morning, although she did not have the exact time. It was now mid-afternoon, certainly things should be tied up by now. She shot him a quick message.

Hey, handsome! How did things go today?

There wasn't an immediate response. It took nearly an hour before she heard from him.

It didn't go well, sexy. Lots of things were covered up and it's going to cost me about 40 grand a year in lost revenue.

Stephanie was very surprised. She knew Daniel was very diligent when acquiring a new business. This was very out of character.

How did this happen?

Daniel:

They hid things very well. I have to see if I want to let it go or push through the courts.

Stephanie:

That doesn't sound good. I guess you need to weigh everything and see how to progress.

Daniel:

You know I will. I'm going to grab a drink with the attorney and then head to the picnic. Have a great night!

Stephanie:

Thank you!

He was taking that better than expected. She knew he did not like to be used or played for a fool. She was willing to bet that unless it would be cost prohibitive, they would be seeing him in court.

She finished out her day and headed home. Brianna was once again out with her friends. Would she ever get used to be an empty nester? It certainly would take time. She made herself a bowl of soup and changed quickly as it cooled.

She wrote in her journal after dinner.

Oh, how quickly things change. Just when I think everything is going well, a wrench gets thrown into the works. Is it really too much to ask for things to be normal? I realize I'm not normal, but I think I'd settle for a little less crazy. I am trying to figure out what lesson is to be learned here. Am I supposed to be less jealous? Should I give up this fantasy of the "happily ever after" that constantly plays through my mind? I just don't get it. I do what I think is right and it goes so wrong. Should I do the opposite of what I think is correct next time? I just wish I had the answers. Going through this shit just really sucks. The pain over the weekend was horrible. I felt like my heart was being ripped out of my chest. I can't remember ever having that feeling in my life. I keep asking myself what have I done in my life that I am now paying for. I honestly cannot remember anything. Granted, I know I am far from perfect, but this must have been a huge sin. Maybe I should just stop trying. Maybe I'm too nice. It certainly seems like the bitchier women aren't used like this. So much for – treat others the way you want them to treat you. I don't recall treating him like a piece of shit. Oh contraire, I put him on a fucking pedestal that he clearly did not deserve. How was I so stupid? This is the part I just don't understand, that and the part where I still want this man. Well, I am going to meet with him day after tomorrow. This time I will be in charge. I have questions that I want answered. After I get my answers, I am going to seduce him, then I will step back to see what happens. If I give it everything I have and I still lose, then I know it wasn't about me. In twenty years I don't want to find myself asking what if I would have. I need to know that I did everything I could, I gave it my all. I will do this and let the chips fall as they may. This is out of my control—it will be what it shall be.

She put down her journal and began thinking about what she wanted to know from him. She took out her laptop and began typing away...

Do you think people won't like you if you show them who you really are?

Above board means that you tell the women there are other women and not let them think they can get you. I think you need to continue to remind them that they are not the only one. After a period of time and a length of intimacy it is just assumed that this is going to be a relationship.

Why do you think all women are users?

What would it take for you to believe a woman to be telling you the truth regarding her feelings and how she handles her relationships?

What is with the "someone my own age?" Your father has a wife 20 years younger, does she not love him? Does she just want his money?

Are there women your age that can keep up with you sexually?

Are you afraid that a younger woman will throw you to the curb in your time of need?

What do you want? Have you written it down?

What makes you self-sabotage when it comes to relationships?

Why do you judge all women based on your wife?

Why don't you believe the right woman is out there?

What is the average time you spend with a woman? What ends it for you?

How many are there now?

Do you find it difficult to keep them straight?

Does it take a lot of your time to keep the balls in the air?

Do you talk to them about your family?

Are there any that you would be upset to lose?

Which other woman sees you for more than just your cock, let me rephrase, a rich cock?

Which ones have you become jealous of?

We have been together over two years, have I ever acted in a way different from what I agreed to?

You talk about having been a Dominant, and our relationship began that way, don't lie, it changed, but it was based on trust, honesty, and respect, what happened last week violated all those rules, can you explain?

You tell me you read all the letters I sent you, how can you say you did not know how I felt?

Why do you push me away? What are you afraid of?

Why can't you open yourself up to a relationship?

Do you really think you can be monogamous?

Do you, in your heart of hearts, want to be happy?

She stopped and read over the questions. Damn, she missed her calling to be an attorney. I guess that's the woman scorned she was channeling.

She closed the computer when she heard the front door closing. Brianna was home, time to be a mom.

Stephanie and Brianna had a few minutes of chit chat before Brianna decided to head to her room. She had a little bit of homework to complete, and it was already getting late.

Stephanie tidied up the kitchen and living room before heading to bed. She wasn't very tired, so she grabbed a book from her office and piled the pillows against the headboard to read until she felt she would be able to drift off.

A few chapters into the book, she began to get drowsy. She placed the book on the nightstand, then went to check on Brianna.

Although the light in her room was still glowing, Brianna was fast asleep. Stephanie turned off the light and quietly pulled the door closed. She remembered doing the same thing for the baby girl that used to occupy this room. Where had all those years gone? In a handful of months, this room would be empty. Stephanie's life had changed so much in the past few years, and they were going to change even faster in the months to come.

She returned to her room, turned out the light, and sent Daniel a good night text before snuggling under the covers. She fell asleep just moments later.

♦

She was just finishing her makeup when Daniel sent his first text.

Good morning, gorgeous! Are you ready for tomorrow?

He had no idea how ready she was. Not only had she written out the questions, she had played through her mind exactly what she would do to him in her seduction. He would not know what hit him.

Good morning, handsome! I am very ready for tomorrow, I just hope you are…

Daniel:

That sounds ominous. Should I be afraid? You aren't bringing any whips, are you?

Always a sense of humor in the face of a challenge. He knew there was a reason for her visit, and it was not anything he was prepared to deal with.

I do not own a whip, but if you would like me to get one, I can certainly stop on my way.

Daniel:

No, no, no. I am not into pain, just pleasure.

Stephanie:

That's what I have planned. What time should I come over?

She would be taking the lead; he was not going to be in charge tonight.

Would 6:30 work for you?

Stephanie:

That will work. I will see you then. Have a great day!

She was turning the tables. She would no longer be drug along on his schedule. She did not have time to play games this morning. She needed to get in the office and get ahead of her clients. She was taking a week off, which meant double the work this week.

She began digging into files as soon as she got into the office. She and Pam worked diligently throughout the morning. It was almost noon when she got a call from Zachary.

"Well, hello there! I wasn't expecting a call, is something wrong?" Stephanie spoke as she got up and closed her office door.

"No, beautiful, there is nothing wrong. I just wanted to go over next week and it's just quicker to talk than text."

"I agree. So, what do I need to know?"

"I have arranged for my plane to fly you in. There will be a driver sent to pick you up at 7 am. As soon as they get you to the airport, the plane will bring you to LA. I am not sure if I will be able to meet you at the airport, but my driver will be there.

We are still working on the exact timelines during your time with us. I want to get as much accomplished as possible without wearing you out. I would like to put in a little downtime at the house for us."

"That sounds lovely. It's so cold here, a little time in the sun will be fabulous. Is there anything I need that would be out of the ordinary?"

"No, as always, I will have everything here for you. I hate to ask a woman this question, but have there been any changes to the measurements we have for you?"

Stephanie laughed out loud, "That is a tough question for a man to ask a woman. As far as I know, I have not put on any winter weight. I've been too busy to get caught up in too much comfort food."

"That's great. I've had my people making you a few outfits, but thought I should double check before we go any further.

On a personal note, how did things go with the college last weekend?"

Question of Trust

"It was wonderful. I think we both fell in love with it. She applied and now we wait to hear their decision. She said they told her it would take at least two weeks. I guess we will have an answer when I get back."

"I'm sure they will take her. She seems to be a good student. I know her mother raised her properly. How could they say no?"

"I think so too, but I don't make the decision. If it happens, it was fate. She will go to the school she is supposed to go to. I've been giving a lot of things to the higher power. Fighting your fate is tiring."

"Sounds like things have not been going well. Anything you need to talk about?"

"No, I've just been soul searching recently. My path is a bit foggy, I'm trying to let go and hopefully the road will clear."

"Well I hope your time away next week will not add to the fog. You know if I could blow it away, I would."

"Yes, I do. You are a very sweet man. I am blessed to have you in my life. Thank you for being so kind."

"Stephanie, I am not being kind, I am being human. You deserve the things I give you. I don't feel that I give more than I receive. I actually don't feel I give you enough."

Stephanie let that last sentence sink in. Would she ever hear that from Daniel? She gave much more to Daniel then she had to Zachary. Although the men were similar, there were a few areas where their differences were deafening.

"Please don't feel that way. I appreciate everything you have done for me and I do not feel in the least bit slighted. I can't imagine a more perfect gentleman."

"Thank you, you are too kind. I am going to let you get back to work. I'm sure you have things to do before next week. Have a productive day. I will see you next week."

"Thank you, good bye."

"Good bye."

She put the phone down. She shook her head and thought – Why can't I just take the pieces of each and make the one I want?

She didn't spend more than a moment on that thought

191

before getting back into work. Pam ordered lunch to be delivered. They ate at their desks, up to their elbows in work.

The rest of the day passed quickly. It was nearly seven before Stephanie decided to call it a night. She went home to her empty house. Brianna had been asked to do some babysitting, and with college around the corner, she was making money every chance she could.

Stephanie spent a quiet evening with some hot chocolate and a few files she had brought home. She was a workaholic, but it's all she knew. She did not come from a privileged family. She knew it took hard work to get what she wanted. She was willing to pay the price.

She checked in with Brianna after ten. The parents were on their way home and she would be back at the house in less than half an hour. Stephanie was satisfied and went upstairs to get ready for bed.

She did not lay her head on the pillow until Brianna was home safe and sound in the room across the hall. She had a big day tomorrow, she needed her rest.

CHAPTER 23

THE DAY HAD BEEN SO BUSY that she really had not taken notice how quiet he had been. She had not heard more from him than his morning text. Nonetheless, she was full steam ahead with her plan. She had left work at four to go home and get ready. She had no sooner left her driveway when she got a message.

Should I just be naked?

Stephanie:

No. I have plans…

Daniel:

Lol…well I could be napping in the fun room…

And so the power struggle begins.

Then I will call you down when I get there.

Daniel:

The front door is open.

This is how things always went with him. He never allowed her to say what she needed to say or ask the questions she needed to ask. He would always shut her down. Tonight was going to be different. She was going to hold her own. She was armed with her questions and she was hell bent on them being answered.

She parked her car in the driveway and walked in the house. She checked in the living room and kitchen, no Daniel. Then she got a message.

Did you call me? Are you in my house?

Stephanie:

No, I did not call you, but I just walked in. I'll wait for you to come down.

He took his good old time sauntering down the stairs and

walking toward her. She was patiently waiting for him. She did not have the excited look on her face that was always there when she saw him. He knew she meant business.

He took her into his arms and began kissing her. There was a different passion behind them tonight. They felt more forceful. He had her in his arms and was not letting go. She struggled to get away, but he fought her.

She finally freed herself, "That's not the way I want to do this," she said when she stepped away. "I want to talk first."

Daniel had an attitude about him, "So you can break up with me?"

Stephanie's face contorted into disbelief, "So I can break up with you? What the hell are you talking about?"

"That's why you came here. To tell me we are over."

"I did not. I just want to talk to you."

He came to her, placing his arms around her, "We will talk, let me put my dick into your pussy first."

Stephanie had no idea what the hell this was about. She had never seen him like this. Why did he think she was breaking up with him? She had not given him any reason to think such a thought. And if that was the case, why was he acting as though he didn't want that to happen?

Stephanie was confused, but she knew the game he was playing. It was all about the control. She cleared her head and got it in the game.

He whispered in her ear, "Drop your pants and turn around, let me put my cock in your cunt."

Her face was now stern. She would be in control. The conversation in her mind went like this... Fine, you want to play that card, I'll let you dip your dick, but you aren't going to cum.

She turned and lowered her trousers. He slid his penis out the leg of his shorts and drove it into her in one motion. Again, asserting his control.

His hands were on her hips as he roughly pumped in and out of her. She allowed him to go at it for about two minutes before she pulled away and turned toward him.

"Save the rest for later."

"Are you sure? It may not be hard later."

"I'll worry about that," she pulled up her pants. "Now, let's sit on the sofa and talk."

He fixed his shorts and went into the living room with her. They sat at opposite ends of the sofa, facing each other.

Stephanie had not grabbed her notes out of her purse, but she knew the questions to ask. She began.

"I'm not sure what that was all about. What has been going on with you?"

"I have been doing a lot of thinking recently. I know you don't understand why I want someone closer to my age, but there are many reasons. We would have more in common and things to talk about. We would have grown up during the same times and listened to the same music."

What the fuck? Did he not think that she could have had aunts and uncle who would have listened to that music? Did he think she was like kids now that listened to Baby Mozart? Fuck no! Her mother was the oldest and when she was with the extended family they listened to the radio and danced to the current music. She knew the Beatles as a group and Beetles as an automobile her youngest aunt drove. Yes, she might have been a toddler during the age of "free love," but she certainly understood the times.

"So you don't feel that we have things to talk about?"

"No, I'm not saying that. I just think that an older woman would be in the same place in her life as I am. It won't be many years and I will be retiring. I will want to travel and having a younger partner would make that tough."

Oh, she saw where this was going. He had already married off his children and she was working on getting hers into college. He had already been a grandfather a few times over, she wasn't even close, or so she hoped.

"So, you really think you will retire? I can't imagine you being completely retired, you would be bored. There is only so much golf you can play before that gets old. You need to keep your finger on the pulse or you would go crazy.

That being the case, how much travelling would you be doing? Don't you think she could go on vacations? Would you really want her up your ass all the time?"

He laughed. "I do enjoy your sense of humor. I don't know what I would do without it. I am very comfortable with you. You are the person I trust the most. There are just so many other things that go into a relationship. I'm sure you understand."

"I do understand what goes into a relationship. It's about give and take. It's about both people getting what they are looking for from the other. It takes a lot to find that one person who can give you everything all tied up in a little bow."

"You're right. But if you find that person, you should not let them go."

HELLO!!! I am fucking right here!!! Okay, I'm not wearing a bow right now, although there might be one on my bra, but for Christ sake, what are you not seeing?!? Damn this man made her so frustrated. His words and actions were far from congruent. She found herself constantly asking what things meant every time she talked to him. It drove her batshit crazy. This man didn't need monogamy, he needed therapy!

She realized there were no other questions that she could ask that were going to get her the answers she needed. There was only one thing left to do.

She stood and put her hand out to him. He took it and began following her up the stairs. She took him into his master bedroom, not the fun room they would always go to. She was making a statement, she was owning him.

He tried to touch her, but she would not allow it. She shook her head slightly and he stopped.

She began by running her hands over his torso. Her moves were slow and calculated. She had played them over in her mind many times. She slid her hands under his t-shirt, hooking the hem in her pinkies, and began pushing it up over his head. She followed his arms with her hands, and when she had pushed it over their hands, she entwined hers in his.

The top had fallen to the floor. Their hands were still above their heads as she began circling them down to his hips, she released them and ran her fingertips across his stomach, over his chest and placed her palms onto him when she got to his shoulders.

Her open hands pushed up his neck and came to rest on his cheeks. She pulled him in and kissed him gently, little pecks on his lips, cheeks, nose, and eyelids. She was on her tip toes when she placed her lips on his forehead.

She kept her hands flat on him as she began to slowly squat in front of him. Her fingers grabbed his elastic waistband and tugged them to the floor. With her hands on his hips, she began nudging his cock with her nose. She nuzzled her face between his thigh and groin.

She looked up at him. She knew he was expecting her to take his cock in her mouth, but this time he would be mistaken. She stood and began a slow strip tease. She was silently playing a song in her head and her movements were in time with it.

Her hips moved as her hands stroked her body. It continued to move as she began removing her shirt. A slow unbutton, little by little revealing her white bra underneath. It lingered on her shoulders until she gradually allowed it to slide down her arms and fall to the floor.

She unhurriedly danced before him. She leisurely began unzipping her pants. She turned and began to wiggle out of them, revealing her bum inch by inch. She was not wearing panties, everything was revealed when she bent over, placing her hands on the floor, and gyrating her ass in the air.

Before she stood, she stepped out of her slacks, spreading her legs wide in front of him. All he could do is watch. She straightened and turned to face him. She placed her hands behind her back and unhooked her bra. She turned to the side and flicked a strap off as her breasts were held in her other arm. She twisted to the other side and repeated.

She stood in front of him holding a cup in each hand. She bounced them up and down before pulling it forward and releasing her large mounds. She stood naked in her pumps as she motioned him to get on the bed.

While he got comfortable, she went into the bathroom in search of some massage lotion. She opened a few drawers before finding something that would suffice. She walked back into the bedroom.

Daniel was lying face down in the middle of the bed. She crawled onto the bed and straddled his buttocks, still in her pumps. She leisurely began her massage at his neck and shoulders. Lazily rubbed his back and worked her way to his butt.

She moved her knees down to his calves. She placed her hands on his cheeks and spread them wide. She bent forward and stuck out her tongue. She began licking his anus and pushing her protrusion inside.

He moaned with delight. He had suggested that she toss his salad many times, and she always refrained. This was her last shot, she was giving it everything. She manipulated his sphincter until her needs got the better of her.

She moved from on top of him and told him to roll over. His cock was hard. She stood it straight up and straddled it. She moaned as she slowly lowered herself onto his dick. She grabbed the top of his headboard and began riding. Her tits were bouncing freely. He grabbed them, placing them in his mouth one at a time.

He continued to nibble and bite her nipples as she rode his dick. He grabbed her hips and began pounding her from the bottom. She was moaning, as was he.

"I want to cum inside you."

"Please do."

He continued driving deep inside her, until he didn't. He had thrust himself into the abyss physically and mentally. They were both panting and vocal in their orgasms.

When they had caught their combined breath, she dismounted and snuggled next to him in bed. She was confident that she had done everything possible. She left nothing on the table. If this did not work, then it was not meant to be.

After fifteen or twenty minutes, they got out of bed and dressed. He walked her to the front door and kissed her good night. She got in her car and began the drive home.

As she drove, tears began filling her eyes. Had she pled her case? Would he see she was the whole package? She didn't know, but she had given it her all. She had no regrets.

When she pulled into her garage, she messaged him that she had gotten home safely. He messaged her good night.

She spent some time with Brianna before heading to her room. Before falling asleep, she began making a list of things she would need for her trip to LA. A few days away right now was a welcomed idea, even if it would be spent working.

CHAPTER 24

ITHAD BEEN A QUIET WEEKEND. Daniel sent a few short messages Friday but was MIA since. She kept herself busy with house cleaning, laundry, and grocery shopping. She wanted the house cleaned and stocked before her trip. She and Brianna had also taken some time to go to a movie, something they had not done for a very long time.

Even though Stephanie had said she was taking the week off, there was one little thing she needed to pop into the office and do. While there, Daniel reached out to her.

Good morning, gorgeous! How is your day going?

Stephanie:

It's going well. Just stopped into the office to do a little something before I leave town.

Daniel:

Leave town? Did this just come up? You didn't mention anything the other night.

Stephanie:

We have been so busy talking about your girlfriend, I didn't think about it. I am flying to LA for a photoshoot. I leave tomorrow morning.

Daniel:

So you will be with Zach. Will he get what I got the other night?

Stephanie:

No one has ever gotten what you got the other night. I'm glad you at least remember, I wasn't sure that you would.

Daniel:

Now, now, no need to be snippy.

Stephanie:

I'm not snippy. I'm upset because I put everything out there and you completely forgot about me this weekend.

Daniel:
Another conversation for another time…enjoy moments okay…
Stephanie:
Is that telling me to be satisfied with the crumbs I get?
Daniel:
Omg… same things happen in my life… I said before if it is unsatisfactory then we can call it quits. Also said I am out of the lifestyle except I would have fun with you if the occasion works for us. Stephanie, please, let's not complicate this. I am dating and you will always be special and I'm here for you as a friend. I'm not looking for new women. You are one of the few people I trust and we have never betrayed each other's trust. Now my boner is gone, back to work. Lol

He just really didn't get it. He wasn't seeing that he was doing anything wrong. If he thought she was going to keep quiet, he was sadly mistaken.

Daniel, I don't want to see you using women like this. This hits a little close to home. I don't want there to be a woman you are dating who thinks she is the only one and then finds out you have had me all along. That's not fair to her.

Daniel:
Omg, such assumptions. WTF? I am honest with women I date, even the one I see the most. Why are all men bad?Details and names are not required but I think this may be a mistake and we should just end the sex part now. I just don't get how women can enjoy men, but men can't enjoy women and the assumption is that it's all sex. I have a dinner date tonight and there won't be sex.

Well maybe he should make sure he tells the "one he sees the most" about that, clearly Stephanie did not have that title. It seemed like there really was someone who was his serious contender.

Can I tell you what happened to a woman I know? She is in love with this man who has not told her about seeing other women. I know you said that they all know there are other women, but when you don't say anything and reinforce that fact then we go into assumption mode, and we are the only one. I am not trying to be combative, I am trying to explain in a way that makes sense to you so you can understand and stay out of trouble.

Maybe you should ask her to define your relationship. If it has been more than a few months, I would be willing to bet that she thinks she will be the next one to carry your name. It's just how our brains work. I know you guys think differently, but women are emotional creatures, not to say that men can't be emotional, it's just different. Take yourself out of the situation and look at it as an outsider. If this was someone else, what would you think? You are the only one with all the information, so you are the only one to come up with the answers. How long have you been with her? Is it making love to her? How upset would she be is she were in the situation I was in last week? Please don't hurt her. Again, I'm not getting in your shit, I'm trying to help you. God knows why, but I still care for you very much.

Her heart was broken. She had given everything she had, and it wasn't enough. Maybe she could at least stop this from happening to someone else.

Okay, I understand. I never want to hurt anyone, ever. I don't understand women falling in love so quickly with me. All those years married and never hearing the word. I want monogamy but don't know if I'm ready. Should have stopped and explained to you sooner. Somehow I thought we could be friends and thought there was such a thing as fuck buddies. I totally screwed up and need to change. After not feeling desired in my marriage and having sex and women fainting over bedroom skills – I feel a bit played. A woman who did cause me a big problem calls me three months after she is with someone and tells me that she needs my cock to be satisfied. WTF? I wrongly thought that we were all over 30 so we were just making adult decisions. I wish I was average in bed so I knew they wanted me. I care about the women I see, but all can't wait to get my pants off. What happened to conversation?

Wow, just wow. She was glad she was sitting down. She wasn't sure if he was really that insecure or a severe narcissist. Yes, he was fantastic in bed, and most men are not, but women passing out? Maybe you should take them out to dinner first, or not have them drink as much. Fuck buddies do just that, they fuck, period, end of sentence. They don't have daily conversations and compliment each other. Did she really have to teach him everything?

I think you are letting your ego get in the way. Yes there is such a thing as friends with benefits but in that situation you talk about the other partners and don't say anything that could be emotional. There's nothing wrong with being monogamous, or monogamish. You are a kid in a candy store right now and if that's what you want, you need to be clear EVERY time. I'm sure it's exciting for you after what you went through in your marriage, but you need to figure out what you want. If you want to be monogamous with this woman, you are screwing yourself right now. If she finds out what has been going on, she could end it. If nothing else, you will have a long climb up to regain the trust.

Why was she doing this? Why was she handing him over to another woman? She must be nuts. She continued.

As far as conversation, what do you tell them upfront? What does your dating profile look like? I hate to say it, but some of them could just be using the sex as a way to get a hold of you because of what you can offer them financially. I understand what you are saying about being used. I think if you honestly took a look at it you would be able to figure out who wanted you for you and who wanted you for just your cock or your money or whatever. You are a very smart man Daniel, but you are still a very hurt man. I don't think you've taken the time that you need to heal. I think a lot of what you are doing is to be busy and avoid having to deal with the layers of shit you have to go through. Please understand, I'm not judging, I'm speaking from experience.

Daniel:

Okay, but the last three or four months have not been fun and not about me. I have tried to make everyone happy my whole life and this has been a nightmare. Only way to find happiness is to stop and give this woman an honest 100% effort. If it doesn't work, then I gave it everything. Thank you, so when should I start?

She was in tears. Her heart had been ripped from her chest; his words were the same she used in her journal about her last time with him. What a cruel joke, but it wasn't a joke, it was reality.

You start now.

She placed her phone on the desk and began to wail. Her cries were deep. This was not what she wanted to hear, and certainly not at the time she wanted to hear it. Tomorrow she would be heading to LA, how would she hide this? How would she put on the happy face with this on her mind?

She pulled herself together, went to the bathroom and cleaned her face. She could not leave the office with red puffy eyes. The world could not see her like this.

The cold water reduced her symptoms. She kept makeup at work, and within minutes she was ready to leave and head home.

As she drove, she thought about what had happened. The man who she thought was the love of her life was gone. She had never felt this empty. Everything she had thought—was now wrong. Nothing made sense to her.

Brianna was home from school before Stephanie returned. They spent a lovely evening together, going out to dinner and doing a little shopping. It was good for Stephanie; that was, until she came home and Brianna went to her room.

From nowhere, tears began streaming down her face. She headed to her room, not wanting to take the chance of Brianna seeing her. She cried for what felt like an eternity. She got herself together as a text came in.

Good evening, beautiful! Looking forward to seeing you tomorrow. I promise not to work you too hard.

She really hoped that he would work her hard. She needed to forget what had happened.

Good evening! I'm excited. I will do what is necessary to get this campaign underway.

Zachary:

I wish all my employees had that attitude. Maybe you can teach them a thing or two.

Stephanie:

I'm sure you have very good people, you are their leader.

Zachary:

Yes, they are good, but they are not you. It's getting late, I will let you get your beauty sleep, not that you need it. Good night.

Stephanie:

Thank you! See you in the morning.

She really did need to get to sleep and prepare for tomorrow. She needed to throw herself into her work now, it was all she had.

Her head hit the pillow, but sleep did not come for quite some time. Her mind kept playing today's loop over and over. Tears dripped onto her bedding. She prayed that tomorrow would be better.

◆

She said good bye to Brianna as she headed to the limo. It was there at seven just as Zachary said it would be. It was a relief to get in the seat and head to the airport. She began to breathe a sigh of relief, until she heard that familiar sound.

Good morning, sexy! Or should I switch to Stephanie?

Stephanie:

You shouldn't use either. That's not giving it 100%.

Daniel:

Oh, no more communication? No stopping by my house? No stimulation?

Stephanie rolled her eyes, was he serious?

Daniel, you made your decision. You want to give her 100%. I'm not going to get in your way. I told you almost two years ago, that if I wasn't going to make the short list, just tell me so I could go with my dignity. I stand by what I said. I always do.

Daniel:

You are a wonderful woman, counselor and friend. Thank you. I know not what you wanted. Have a fabulous day!

She fought back tears, but did not hold back her words.

You know not what I wanted?? I could not have been more clear. I write my feelings and my life in every word. I communicated it to you constantly. At this point it doesn't matter. Please, don't ever tell someone what a good person they are when you are choosing someone else. All you are saying is that they are good, but not good enough for you. If you were unclear, maybe you could have asked questions and really gotten to know me. There are other things I could say, but it doesn't matter. You were put in my life for a reason and a season, not forever.

After she sent the message, she turned off her phone as a tear ran down her cheek. She quickly wiped it away before the driver could catch a glimpse.

She looked out the window and watched as the sun came over the horizon. In a short time, she would be in the sky toward her future. It was time to leave the past behind.

More Books by Melissa Lynn Christian

Question of Ownership

Melissa's Short Stories: Vol. 1

Melissa's Short Stories: Vol. 2

Naples Comes Alive

MelissaLynnChristian.com

www.ingramcontent.com/pod-product-compliance
Lightning Source LLC
Chambersburg PA
CBHW031230260626
47169CB00007B/2233